CAUGHT IN THE RAT RACE!

Before Melvinge's marveling eyes appeared a six-foot-tall rodent in Adidas running shoes and red nylon trunks. It ran on its hind legs with its front legs pumping up and down. A square of paper bearing the digits 22 fluttered against the front of its red fishnet shirt.

"You're all here to watch a rat race?" Melvinge asked in amazement.

"A three-day rat race," the rhino corrected. He turned away and yelled, "Go, Number Twenty-Two!"

A penetrating voice cut through the babble of the crowd before Melvinge could speak again: "Change can be real without being substantial."

Melvinge recognized the voice of the woman with rhinestone sunglasses. He realized, with a sinking feeling, that he would have to go back past her to reach the Outer Space Marines—no problem if she stuck with her current audience. But if she transferred her attention to him, he might find himself in possibly the only thing duller than a three-day rat race: a lecture on metaphysics!

He turned toward her anyway, and started to elbow his way back through the crowd.

NIGHT OF THE LIVING RAT!

DANIEL M. PINKWATER'S
MELVINGE OF THE MEGAVERSE
BOOK 2 • BY DOYLE and MACDONALD

A GLC Book

ACE BOOKS, NEW YORK

Night of the Living Rat! is an original publication of The Berkley Publishing Group. This work has never appeared before in book form.

An Ace Book/published by arrangement with General Licensing Company, Inc.

PRINTING HISTORY
Ace edition / April 1992

A GLC BOOK

Daniel M. Pinkwater's Melvinge of the Megaverse is a trademark of General Licensing Company, Inc.
Cover and logo design by Steve Brenickmeyer.
Cover art by Steve Fastner and Rich Larson.

ISBN: 0-441-91079-3

Ace Books are published by The Berkley Publishing Group, 200 Madison Avenue, New York, NY 10016.
The name "Ace" and the "A" logo
are trademarks belonging to Charter Communications, Inc.

PRINTED IN THE UNITED STATES OF AMERICA

10 9 8 7 6 5 4 3 2 1

Introduction

The Megaverse Mall is the largest shopping mall ever conceived. Centrally located in Time, Space, and the Other (more about the Other in the book itself!) off the Interstate, the Megaverse Mall serves the needs of uncounted life forms from every world and time.

The parking has accommodation for over 178,000,000 vehicles of every description. And there are generally 336,000,000 vehicles cruising for a space.

The average visit to the Megaverse Mall lasts three to four lifetimes, the first of which is spent looking for a parking place, and the last looking for that place again after visiting the Mall. Most visitors never see the Mall, having been distracted by one of the improvised satellite malls, containing only a few thousand emporia. These gypsy malls, erected without permission by freebooters, are demolished by the Megaverse Management

1

Company when they are discovered—generally after thirty or forty years of profitable operation.

Some simple souls go home having seen one of these imposter malls, believing they've seen The Mall. ("See one mall, you've seen The Mall," is a pun incomprehensible to most, which has appeared on bumper stickers for millennia.)

The actual Megaverse Mall is often taken for the Christian heaven. You can get jeans there. There's a cookie shop. A Radio Shack, of course. And a place where you can get sausage products and cheese. And Cinema 100,000.

After perhaps four lifetimes, a family having come to the Mall may make to depart with its newly acquired lava light, waterbed, designer jeans, plastic shoes, rock 'n' roll records—some happy, some sad, some newborn, some dead—but always vowing to come again to the Greatest Mall in Creation.™

In the Parking Lot, murder is common, as is accidental death arising from one life form failing to recognize other life forms as such. Common victims are Germ-people and Pebble-people—and of course Parking-space men are crushed to death in great numbers.

There are periodic raids by pirates and predators (which events are merely rumors in those parts of the Parking Lot where they are not happening), likewise, wars, famines, hurricanes, and plagues.

Because the Megaverse Mall attracts people from not only different places, but also from different times—all times—it's possible that one might meet one's ancestors, and also one's descendents. It's statistically unlikely that one will meet anybody one knows there—yet people do (like in New York City). The complementary theory is that if one were to stay there long enough one would meet everybody there is or ever was or will be, because sooner or later everybody goes there, even people who claim they don't like it.

The Parking Lot is the scene of all the action. It has the aspect of a gigantic fair or encampment. Some of the flavor can be inferred from the following paraphrase from *Slaves of Spiegel*:

Androids, gleptoids, intelligent robots, werewolves, insubstantial thoughtforms, mineral-creatures, astral jellyfish, giant Manx cats, and the clown-men of Noffo are present. There are also musicians and actors, jugglers and acrobats, fortune-tellers and wise men, dancers and swindlers. There are space doctors tending to the ills of every creature from every world. There are barbers who charge according to how many hairs the customer has, and others who charge according to how many heads.

Tents and prefabricated buildings have been erected. Itinerant restaurateurs have set up many sausage stands, pizza parlors, soda fountains, bakeries, candy shops, deep-fried chopped-liver wagons, mayonnaise carts, and bagel factories.

3

Pilgrims and shoppers *cum* merrymakers walk, crawl, hop, slither, fly, and float about, all day and all night, enjoying the many pleasant spectacles. There are roast goose jugglers, meteor swallowers, monsters able to turn themselves inside out, many-mouthed musicians who can play fifteen horns at once, pseudo-octopusian Fandango dancers, and whistlers from Glintnil. There are mixed beast races, wrestling matches against giant slothoids from Neptune, six-dimensional chess games, screaming contests, and the knocking down of three milk bottles with a baseball.

Spontaneous triumphs and parades are common. Also entertainments sponsored by local warlords and politicians. Typically, they begin with gleptillian musicians, glepts, pseudo-glepts and gleptiles from the galaxy of Twilbstein. Each gleptoid is capable of producing the sound for a full ninety-piece symphony orchestra from within his own body. A phalanx of a hundred such musicians, wearing gleptizoidal helmets, might sound the fanfare announcing a spectacle.

Next might come rank upon rank of Freddians. Known for their sweetness, these adorable inhabitants of the planet Fred distribute bouquets of space orchids, onions, and zitzkisberries to the insanely happy crowd, and put everybody in an even better mood—if that is possible.

Giant ducks from a planet of unknown origin are led through the makeshift streets, each duck held by a stout chain in the hands of a powerful Spiegelian pirate. The crowds cheer, the ducks snarl and hiss. The pirate duck-handlers control the fearsome beasts.

A succession of strange and amusing animals is led before the crowd. Fluorescent lizards, singing walruses, lighter-than-air bears, wombats (both wild and domesticated)—these and many other rare zoological specimens are presented to the enthralled spectators.

Next come famous people: foreign dignitaries, ambassadors from other worlds, heroes, celebrities, newscasters, athletes, and interplanetary rock stars.

Here is Rolzup, the Martian High Commissioner, a great favorite of the crowd. Here is the Ugly Bug Band, a famous rock group of which all the members are ugly bugs. Here is Dr. Kissinger, the reincarnated Attila the Hun, the Three Stooges, and the ghostly form of Alexander the Great.

If the spectacle is by way of celebration of a victory in war, or the arrival of a band of pirates, there may be an exposition of plunder and captives.

That's why everyone's going to the Megaverse Mall.

For now, let's tune in on a certain Time, Space, and the Other vehicle, and listen as the story unfolds. . . .

Chapter 1

The Hideous Genesis of Keester Button

Who loves that slothoform, man oh man,
Amorphoid fleshopod, man oh man.
                              —Blind Grapefruit

Sid the amorphoid fleshopod pulled back on the whistle lever, and chortled to hear the nail-squeaking scream. He was cruising down the Interstate in a shiny new Plonkomatic which some poor fool had left in the parking lot at Pinkie's Chili Dog Stand. Left it there with the keys in the ignition and its pseudobrain in neutral, so that even a mostly honest businessman with a recently extruded head sticking out of his side could get it going and be gone.

Sid flipped on the Plonkomatic's hyperradio for some drive-time music, and reached into the cooler beside him on the front seat. He'd packed the cooler as soon as he'd decided to abandon his roadside chili dog stand and taco parlor, minutes after Sdark the Loan Shark had bitten off his pound of flesh—a pound of flesh bearing an uncanny resemblance to Sid's head.

"Good thing for me Loan Sharks don't know

7

a whole lot about us fleshopods," Sid chortled again—though in fairness to Sdark, one should probably state that his ignorance was a failing shared by 99.44 percent of the known population of the Megaverse. Sdark, in attempting to bite off Sid's head, had merely gotten an extruded pseudopod which (only temporarily) looked like the head in question.

Thinking back on the incident prompted the fleshopod to give his interior colloids a shrug, thus moving the current quasi-head from his side to a new placement atop his torso, one better suited to watching for highway signs. That minor adjustment taken care of, Sid pulled a kumquat-and-cream-cheese sandwich from the cooler and started to munch on it. A folk show was on the radio, part of a program called "Mall Things Consistent" on NPR (Naturally Pathetic Reception). Today's show featured an old-time blues singer named Blind Grapefruit, who was singing a slow ballad to the accompaniment of a steel-string guitar. Blind Grapefruit had the sort of voice that made it clear why things like music lessons, re-recording, overmastering and studio dubbing had been invented.

Melvinge's heading for the Mall
Trying to buy some shoes,
He stopped in a Low-rent Parking Lot
And got them Gypsy Blues.

The dog named Harlan rescued him
Then they stopped for a bite to eat,

But Mel was the bite that Sdark ate
Like a nickel candy treat.

Mel met with Ratner, his loving dad,
Within the Loan Shark's guts,
They got away in the Grabovnikon
The Loan Shark he said "Nuts."

Mel got an earring, a pretty thing,
And met with Loola too,
But Larry shot him in the heart,
And Volume One was through.

The song continued as Sid pressed down on the interlopal time/space discontinuancer and surged onward to the next segment of the Interstate. The rush of the wind through the quasi-hair of his new head blurred the words of Blind Grapefruit's song—which is a pity, because Sid could have saved himself a lot of trouble by listening.

But with the open road stretching out before him and Sdark the Loan Shark left somewhere far behind, Sid felt too good to care about the background music. "This is the life," he said. "It beats the heck out of flipping hamburgers in someone else's universe."

The thought brought something else to what could laughingly be called Sid's mind. "Speaking of flipping hamburgers in someone else's universe, I wonder how Ratner is doing?"

Sid's erstwhile short-order cook had taken off running into the Goober Dessert chasing Sdark when that Loan Shark departed. So involved was Sid in trying to remember exactly what had happened only that morning (as if it was important[1]), that he drove right past his exit on the Interstate. Missing the exit was entirely his fault, too, since the signs for Satisfaction had started a whole fifteen timeskips before the off-ramp.

But there he was, cruising merrily along in the center lane of the Interstate, and it wasn't until the signs for Confusion started that he realized that he had missed his turn. Then a whole string of Ceratopsians (and one Iguanodon) blocked him from moving over to the right-hand lane, so he couldn't get off at Confusion and just turn around. He managed to get to the right lane just as the exit for Hysteria showed up, but Hysteria was an Exit Left so he missed that one, too.

By now Sid was starting to fume and pound his handoids on the steering gear. A couple of timeskips farther on an exit appeared on the right, and Sid, not bothering to read the sign, took it and was grateful.

The sign, had Sid only looked, bore the ominous legend Hoboken Rejects. Below, in black on yellow, appeared the even more ominous phrase Exit Only.

At the bottom of the off-ramp, Sid found himself in a parking lot. Not just any ordinary parking lot either, but one of the Parking Lots of the Megaverse Mall. Let us leave Sid cruising along,

---

[1]Which of course it was, but not as important in the immediate scheme of things as watching the road might have been.

looking for a parking space, long enough to tell you what the Megaverse Mall is, so that you may appreciate the significance of his current predicament.

The Meg-Universal Mall (to use its full name) is so big that it takes more than one lifetime to visit. Anything that you could possibly want is for sale there, sometimes at two or three locations, all with competitive pricing. Surrounding the Mall are the Parking Lots, parking lots of such intensity that all other parking lots surrounding all other malls in all other universes are mere pale reflections of the Parking Lots of the Megaverse Mall.

In the same way, the Megaverse Mall is the One True Mall, the Master Mall against which the rest are measured and found wanting. If this were not true, all one would have to do to achieve supreme happiness would be to take a plane to the Dallas/Fort Worth metroplex, where shopping malls, some of them quite wonderful, are thick on the ground.

Now, if the Megaverse Mall is vast, the Parking Lots that surround it are vaster still—so vast that, no matter where you park, it is problematic whether you will be able to find the Mall. Rumor has it that the primary activity for many of the billions of beings who have found a place to park is seeking the Mall Entrance (which, you will be happy to learn, has wheelchair access).

We now return to our story, already in progress.

For some time now, Sid had been driving up and down between rows of objects, most of them

11

unnameable and unrecognizable. *It's parked,* Sid thought nervously, looking at something yellow and ovoid resting on the tarmac. *So it has to be a vehicle.*

Then—up ahead—could it be? Next to a rusted-out Studebaker Lark with a "This Car Climbed Mount Washington" sticker on the rear bumper—it was! A parking space!

Sid drove forward and, with a minimum of backing and filling, brought the Plonkomatic to a halt. He shut off the ignition, set the hand brake, the foot brake, and the tail brake, and to make assurance doubly sure, threw out a couple of anchors. Only then did he look around, and what he saw did not bring a smile to his lips and a song to his heart.

He now understood the reason for the near-miraculous existence of this parking space: no one before him had possessed the sheer nerve needed to park here.

Sid, who had parked in this spot out of desperation, now found himself directly adjacent to a Gypsy encampment, a Gypsy encampment which—with its sleazy appearance and unsavory inhabitants—brought new meaning to the word *dubious.* The fact that Sid had fetched up alongside this particular Gypsy encampment, out of all the possible Gypsy encampments in all the possible Parking Lots of the Megaverse Mall, also brings new meaning to the words *incredible coincidence,* but we will let that pass for now.

Instead we will talk of the pound of flesh, the bitten-off head, the piece of his mind that Sdark took from Sid as partial payment for the loan on Pinkie's Chili Dog Stand. Sid was a good skate. A little hideous, slimy, carbuncular, and randomly tufted, true, but still good at heart—or at any rate, not all that much worse than the common run of creaturekind.

Regretfully, the same could not be said for his missing head-shaped pseudopod, rocked in the belly of the beast. For if Sid had been good at heart before his close encounter of the worst kind with Sdark, he had been bad at head. Nearly everyone is partly good and partly bad, but in Sid's case all the naughty bits had concentrated themselves in the now-missing headopod.

That bitten-off appendage was still living when it slid down Sdark's craw and into the nameless horror of the Loan Shark's bloated guts. There, in antediluvian sludge, it regenerated and grew, taking into itself all manner of disgusting glop and bad manners.

At length (for Loan Sharks are huge and the digestive systems of Loan Sharks are dreadfully slow) it became a creature fully as large as was Sid himself, identical to him in every way (that is to say, loathsome), but with one important difference: the Sid-clone was as drained of virtue as an upside-down Coke can. His delight was wickedness, his joy was pain. What do you expect, after growing up on a diet of half-digested halvah and Scooter Pies?

All during the endless weeks the headopod spent swirling and bubbling amid noxious substances, humming "I Ain't Got No Body" and

13

growing ever larger and larger, it also grew a plan. The head—together with its assorted body-shaped extrusions—wanted to find its original owner, and take him back. Merge. Become one. Once again become the master. Be complete.

When eventually this new-grown body passed from Sdark by means that we will not describe here,[2] it found itself in need of a name. "Snuggles," "Bunny," and "Leonard" were instantly rejected as projecting the wrong image. The new-formed body stood on the shores of the great Goober Dessert and gave its primordial yawp at the darkling sky:

"I am Keester!" it shouted. "I am Keester! I am Keester Button!"

With that, Keester began the Long March to the Interstate, famous in song and story. The Long March was followed by the Fair-Sized April, and by the middle of May Keester was on the Interstate itself, near the site of Pinkie's Chili Dog Stand (EZ Off, EZ On).

He walked into Pinkie's fully expecting to find Sid hard at work selling recycled-protein frankfurters and tofu milkshakes to unwary travelers in search of the Megaverse Mall. He found, instead, that the chili dog stand was under new management.

"What happened to the old boss?" Keester demanded.

"The old boss vanished, and left this prime property up for grabs," replied Mortimer O'Malley, the

[2]But which were, trust us, yucky.

14

current owner. He had acquired Pinkie's from Sdark, and now held it under terms of ruinous interest on a mortgage of dubious validity.

Keester scowled, the pseudoflesh of his face furrowing up in ripples. "Any idea where he went?"

"Yeah," piped up a voice from a corner booth. "The fungoid grabbed my Plonkomatic and headed out on the Interstate. I been here ever since, waiting for a ride so's I could look for him."

"Come on," Keester said. "You and me. I want to find that loungewort my own self."

"But we don't have no conveyance," the voice-piper protested. He was a thin character with geeky eyebrows. Anybody looking at him would peg him as someone born to have his car stolen while he was downing a double Venusburger, as in fact had happened.

"Right," snarled Keester. He backed off and thundered a challenge to everyone in Pinkie's: "Who here is going to give me and my pal a ride?"

No one spoke.

"You," Keester snarled, pointing at Mortimer. "You got a vehicle?"

"Yeah," said the new owner of Pinkie's. "But I ain't giving it to you."

"And why might that be?" Keester asked, his voice dangerous and low.

"Because you *are* the old boss," Mortimer replied. "Your face is on wanted posters all over the universe. Wanted for Failure to Pay an Unjust Loan and Aggravated Plonk Theft."

"*My* face?"

"It's on the front of your head," Mortimer said with a shrug. "I suppose it's your face."

"You dimbulb! That's gotta be my clone." Keester reached out one handopod and grabbed Mortimer by the neck. "Give me your timeskipper, or you'll regret it," he bubbled menacingly.

"I regret it already," Mortimer muttered, feeling the rubbery pseudoflesh on his skin. Nevertheless, he pulled out a ring of keys and tossed them at Keester's feet. "It's the pink and blue Spradillac with the Elvis hood ornament."

"Right," said Keester. Then, pointing at the geeky voicepiper, he said, "Come on, you."

Together they strode from the chili dog emporium and out into the parking lot.

"Gee," the geeky one said as they got into the conveyance. "It sure is swell, you taking me along like this."

"Swell nothing," Keester said. "There's only five kazillion Plonkomatics in the universe. You, my friend, are going to tell me which one of them is yours when we find it."

"What makes you so sure we'll find it?"

"Don't worry about that," Keester said, gunning the engine. A nasty grin twisted his features. "You want your Plonkomatic back, don't you? We'll find him. And when we do . . . that's when the fun really starts."

He gunned the Spradillac one more time, then floored it out of the parking lot and onto the Interstate, spraying gravel the whole way.

16

Chapter 2

A Day at the Rat Races

I will not be afraid of death at all,
I said I will not be afraid of death at all,
'Til Melvinge makes it to the Mega Mall.
                          —Blind Grapefruit

Melvinge opened his eyes and sat up.

"Some kind of hero I turned out to be," he muttered. "First I get kidnapped, then I get turned into a werewolf, and then I get shot to death with a silver bullet by a band of ticked-off gypsies. And all before I could find True Love, the Meaning of Life, and the Megaverse Mall."

Melvinge looked about him at the surrounding landscape, and wished at once that he hadn't. "Why is it," he demanded of the smoggy and unfeeling sky, "that the afterlife looks just like Trenton, New Jersey?"

Prior to his recent unfortunate demise, Melvinge had been a resident of Time, Space, and the Other—that bundle of universes inhabited by most of the intelligent and not-so-intelligent creatures of the cosmos. Mostly Melvinge had stayed in Time and Space, although once or twice he had received visitors from the Other. But since this

17

place clearly wasn't his native Time and Space, nor yet the Other, Melvinge figured that he was probably in the Neitherworld.

Another quick look around, and his guess proved all too accurate. In the middle distance, a dark iron railway trestle over a sludgy river bore a soot-smudged sign reading The Megaverse Makes, The Neitherworld Takes. Underneath, in Day-Glo Orange spray paint, a graffiti artist had informed the world that Abraxas Was a Fink.

Melvinge pulled himself to his feet. Being dead, he promptly discovered, tended to upset your equilibrium a bit at first. He leaned for balance against the rough brick wall of the nearest building, a run-down eatery with "Riverfront Spamshop" painted on its front window in peeling red letters.

The unmistakable odor of Trenton Spam Chowder wafted out through the open door, blended with another aroma that Melvinge identified, after some thought, as the Spam Plate Orgy advertised on a placard in the Spamshop window. The combination smelled like a mixture of lard and dishwater. Melvinge realized, with a wave of mingled gratitude and nausea, that being dead meant he'd never be hungry again—a good thing, given the local cooking.

He turned his back on the Riverfront Spamshop and set out on foot, heading away from the river toward what he hoped was downtown. So far, he hadn't seen anything that looked like another living being—which stood to reason, he reflected, if the Neitherworld was where dead

18

things went. But after a little while, as he wandered through the grimy streets and back alleys of the Neitherworld, he heard voices, mixed with cheers and the sound of running footsteps.

He rounded a corner, and saw that the block ahead was choked with people and other, more unlikely, beings.[1] All of them stood with their backs to Melvinge, their attention fixed on something that he couldn't see.

The noise of pounding feet came from somewhere beyond the crowd, moving from right to left along what Melvinge supposed was a crossing street. He wished that the gypsies had let him live long enough to grow only a little taller, so that he could see what was going on before he got there. Since growing taller soon was out of the question, he hit the back of the crowd and started elbowing his way toward the front.

"Even those who deny the reality of substance have to admit the reality of accidents," said a voice in the crowd.

Somehow, thought Melvinge, the voice sounded—well, not familiar, exactly, but significant, as if he really ought to glance in that direction. He glanced, and saw a woman with a henna-red bouffant hairdo and rhinestone sunglasses. She had one fist clenched around the

---

[1] Roughly 50 percent of the onlookers, as it happened, belonged to species other than *homo sapiens*—lynxes, sphinxes, manticores, allosaurs, pteranodons, and even the occasional amorphous slothoform (although those tended to look mostly human until their concentration slipped).

19

forelimb of a rhinoceros in a four-piece suit.[2]

Except for pulling his hoof away from her vise-like grip, the rhino in the four-piece suit ignored her. "Here comes Number Forty-Three!" it bellowed.

The pounding footsteps approached from the right and faded away to the left. The crowd broke into shouts of encouragement.

Melvinge pushed his way past the rhinoceros (although not without some effort), and fetched up against a blue-painted sawhorse with the words Polite Line—Never Cross stenciled on it in yellow. Another line of sawhorses blocked the street on the other side of the crossing, with another crowd pushing up against it facing him. From the other side, behind the opposite Polite Line, a Golden Guernsey yelled, "Here comes Twenty-Two!"

More running footsteps approached. Then before Melvinge's marveling eyes appeared a six-foot-tall rodent in Adidas running shoes and red nylon trunks. It ran on its hind legs with its front legs pumping up and down as it ran. A square of paper bearing the digits 22 fluttered against the front of its red fishnet T-shirt. The huge creature pounded up the road, its tongue lolling from its gasping mouth, its tiny pink eyes glazed. The crowd around Melvinge raised up a hoarse, half-human cheer.

Melvinge turned to the rhinoceros in the four-

_____

[2]Pants, jacket, vest, and bow tie—the height of fashion on the planet Cribbage Four in the Whirlpool Galaxy.

piece suit. "You're all here to watch a rat race?" he asked in amazement.

"A three-day rat race," the rhino corrected. He turned away and yelled, "Go, Number Twenty-Two!"

Melvinge noted how the rat's naked tail protruded from an elastic-rimmed hole in the back of its trunks. When the rat was out of sight, he looked back at the rhinoceros beside him. "I can't imagine anything more boring than a three-day rat race."

"Stick around the Neitherworld for a while," the rhino advised him. "Boredom is an art form around here."

Melvinge took this in for a moment. "I don't want to be difficult," he said finally, "but I can't see spending my afterlife watching a rat race."

"Go tell it to the Marines," said his companion, and went back to watching for the next rat runner to appear.

A penetrating voice cut through the babble of the crowd before Melvinge could speak again. "Change can be real without being substantial."

Melvinge recognized the voice of the woman with the rhinestone sunglasses. She had captured another unfortunate (a yak-herder this time, with his string of yaks lined up on the pavement beside him) and was shouting in his ear. Melvinge wasn't surprised to see, over the horned heads of the yaks, a squad of men in the dazzling red-and-gold uniform of the Outer Space Marines.

"There must be a reason for things," the woman insisted to the yak-herder, who wasn't listening. Her beehive hairdo bobbed with each syllable.

Melvinge realized, with a sinking feeling, that he would have to go back past her to reach the Marines—no problem, if she stuck with her current audience. But if she transferred her attentions to *him*, he might find himself trapped in possibly the only thing duller than a three-day rat race: a lecture on metaphysics. He turned toward her anyway, and started to elbow.

"Here comes Ninety-Eight!" shouted someone behind him, but Melvinge didn't bother to look. Instead, he pushed on back through the crowd.

"Reality," the woman said as Melvinge came up to her, "contains both the possible and the actual." Her sentence turned into an "Ooof!" as Melvinge's elbow caught her in the solar plexus. Then he was past her and closing in on the squad of Marines.

"Ah, sir," he said in a hopeful tone to the first Marine he came to, "what is there to do around here? For fun, I mean. Other than watching rat races, that is."

"Most of us," the Marine replied, "play cards."

Melvinge brightened. He'd never amounted to much of a cardplayer back in Time and Space, but here in the Neitherworld, the rules might be different. "Where can I go to find a game?"

"By the right flank, march!" the Marine replied. "Three hundred meters down the street, turn right. Forward, march! Two hundred fifty feet, eyes left. Up the stairs. Half left, past the third trash can, turn right. Six feet, to the right oblique, march! Second door on the left, *not* the green door, knock eight times, say 'Moolie sent me.' "

"Ah, thank you, sir," Melvinge said, more confused than he'd been at any time since the night he'd missed his exit on the Interstate and wound up in the Macaroni System, and him without a road map. "Very kind of you. Can't thank you enough . . ."

"Never mind the thanks!" barked the Marine. "Repeat the instructions!"

Chapter 3

The Quest Continues

When the women heard that Melvinge was dead,
  They went back home and they outed in red.
Come slippin' and slidin' up and down the street,
  In their loose Mother Hubbards and their stocking
    feet.

—Blind Grapefruit

Let us leave Melvinge wandering the streets of the Neitherworld in search of a game of luck and skill, and return to the Parking Lots of the Megaverse Mall, where abandoned cars from all the farthest reaches of the cosmos stretch out from horizon to horizon.

Also stretched out in this Parking Lot, at this particular moment, was Melvinge—or at least the mortal remains of him—lying dead on the litter-strewn tarmac with a silver-bullet hole in his heart, and Harlan the faithful dogoid (*homo arfia*) making moan over his boss's body.

"Oh, fudge," Harlan moaned—rhetoric had never been his strong point. "Oh, *fudge!*"

This was certainly not the sort of thing that a real sidekick would have allowed his boss to get into. A real sidekick would have leapt into the path of the bullet and taken the hit himself. A real sidekick would have felt his own life a cheap price to pay to save the hero. A real sidekick would have delivered a touching farewell speech before succumbing in the hero's arms.

Then the hero would rise to his feet, the line of his jaw set in manly determination (with perhaps a hint of moistness in his steely eyes, to show sensitivity), and go forth to do some serious tail-kicking among the bad guys who had shot his pal.

"I really screwed that one up," Harlan muttered. He kicked the toe of one booted hindpaw into the crumpled Popsicle wrappers littering the pavement of the Parking Lot. "Now what do I do?"

No mystic voice answered. Instead came the hoarse whisper of Snake-Spit the gypsy thug: "Five bucks for five minutes alone with your friend."

The dogoid paused for a moment, considering. A whole fiver in hard currency? He shrugged. What the heck, Melvinge was dead anyway.

"Okay," he replied, then shot out a forepaw to stop Snake-Spit from hurrying past. "Not so fast, bwana. Cash in advance."

Muttering a lurid curse involving fleas and armpits, Snake-Spit pulled out a soggy but still legal greenback and handed it to Harlan. The dogoid pocketed it and turned his face upward, ignoring the thug once again. "Why, why, can anyone tell me why?" he demanded of the universe.

While Harlan was declaiming to the sky, Snake-Spit was hard at work on the earring that Melvinge's pathetic, bleeding corpse wore in its right ear. When the thug's first attempts to unfasten the earring proved futile, he drew forth a tremendous clasp knife and cut off the entire ear. He returned the clasp knife to his pocket, then stood and sauntered off.

"I'll avenge you, dear master, never fear," Harlan was saying as Snake-Spit strolled past, casually tossing and catching an earring-studded ear as he went.

"Thanks, pal," Snake-Spit said, not breaking stride.

"Any time," Harlan nodded. "Y'all come back, you hear?"

Then once again Harlan turned his attention to Melvinge's body where it lay (now minus one of its ears) on the pavement of the Megaverse Mall Parking Lot.

"Oh Master, dear Master, I will never desert you!" he cried, going down on one knee beside Melvinge and raising one of the corpse's limp and chilly hands to his doggy lips. "I will take you with me wherever I go, until at last I find a wizard, healer, or holy man who can restore you to life!"

"Hey, give me a hand here," said a new voice. A finger tapping him on the shoulder emphasized the words. Harlan turned.

"Oh, it's you, Ratner," he said to the scruffy middle-aged man in the greasy apron of a short-order cook. "What do you need?"

"Come on," urged Ratner. "Give me a hand and we'll carry him back to the Grabovnikon. It's the

27

Megaverse Mall or bust!"

"Let's not hold our breaths, guys," said Harlan, picking up one of Melvinge's feet. Loola the Gypsy Princess grabbed Melvinge by the other leg, and Ratner picked up the recently defunct hero by the shoulders. Staggering under their burden, they reached the door to the Grabovnikon—which, although it looked like nothing so much as a head-on collision between a Recreational Vehicle and the Fully Automated Kitchen of Tomorrow, was actually the Time/Space Machine that had brought them forth from the innards of Sdark the Loan Shark and into this sorry pass.

"Hey," Harlan said as they reached the door. "Something just occurred to me. We have a parking spot. If we start driving around, we may lose it and never find another."

"Good point," Loola agreed. "Do you have a plan?"

"Always," said Harlan.

"What is it?" Ratner asked, an eager light in his piggy blue eyes.

"We all head out in different directions," said Harlan, "and look for the Mall. Whoever finds it can come back to this parking spot and wait for the others. Do you follow me?"

"Follow you?" said Loola the Gypsy Princess. "I'm way ahead of you. If we *don't* find the Mall, we head back here anyway, and wait for the one who found the Mall to show up and lead us there."

"Which ways do we go?" Ratner asked.

"Melvinge being dead like he is," said Harlan, "there's only three of us. So one of us goes to the east, another goes to the west, and the last one goes to the south."

"What about the north?" Loola asked.

Harlan shook his head. "There is nothing to the north."

The three questers stood about for a moment in awkward silence.

"After you," Harlan said, courteously bowing to Loola.

"No, no, after *you*," Loola demurred. When it came right down to it, she wasn't all that eager to leave the comparative safety and comfort of the Gypsy encampment.

"I insist, ladies first," Harlan proclaimed, waving farewell with a lace handkerchief that he kept tucked in his coatsleeve for just such emergencies. When you come down to it, he wasn't all that hot himself on cruising off into the unknown.

Ratner watched the two of them in amazement. Finally, when the farewells going back and forth between Loola and Harlan showed signs of moving into extra innings, the former short-order cook muttered, "All right then, I'm gone," and started out southward.

Ratner's abrupt departure broke up the chain reaction of politeness. Loola gestured at Melvinge's corpse with her thumb.

"How about him?" she asked.

Harlan hoisted the silent clay onto his back. "I'm taking him with me."

The Gypsy Princess and the faithful dogoid shook hands and went off silently and separately into the dark.

Chapter 4

Kibitzers of the Neitherworld

Oh, Sdark, you Loan Shark,
  I know just the same
You're going to the Neitherworld
  To play a different game.

—Blind Grapefruit

"Got any eights?" said Wild Bill Hickok.

Melvinge yawned. "Go Fish."

Being dead and in the Neitherworld, Melvinge had long since decided, was much like being alive and stuck for the weekend in Paramus, New Jersey. Sure you were there, but who cared? He reached up to scratch his ear—or rather, the place where his ear used to be—and tried to think a coherent thought.

He'd found the gambling hall easily enough— the Marine had neglected to mention the "This Way to the Card Game" signs every five meters— and he'd been playing now for what seemed like forever. The game bored him silly, and so did the people around him (Wild Bill, Xenophon, a couple of United States Vice Presidents, and assorted others) but there was nothing else Melvinge could do. He sat and played the eternal game of Go Fish, and tried to keep his memories.

I am Melvinge, he reassured himself. *No matter what anybody calls me. I am Melvinge.*

He'd been having some trouble with that lately. When he'd first joined the card game, someone, probably Hannibal Hamlin, though it might have been Alexander the Great, had looked over at him and said, "Hi, Vinnie—still missing that ear, huh?"

That was the first time he'd noticed that he'd lost an ear. Or perhaps he'd only misplaced it. Maybe it was under his bed back home, wherever home was.

In any case, the greeting had started a long discussion among the card players about whether or not Melvinge was Vincent Van Gogh, the artist. Every argument Melvinge used—even "Listen, Van Gogh is shorter than I am and speaks Dutch"—met with the irrefutable statement, "Yeah, but you don't have one of your ears."

Melvinge reached up and felt, and sure enough his right ear was gone. The discovery hadn't upset him (at least not much, since he was still mostly certain that he wasn't Van Gogh) but he did get a bit uneasy when he couldn't remember what had happened to the missing ear. He knew that he'd had both ears as recently as, as, oh . . . which brings us to Melvinge's second problem.

The Neitherworld was so mind-numbingly dull that it was driving him stupid.

The same thing had happened to everyone else, too. At Melvinge's left, for instance, sat Rasputin, the Annoyed Monk of Russia, drinking hot tea out of a water glass and glowering at his hand

32

of cards. Melvinge would have loved to have a chat with Rasputin about, well, anything. But all Rasputin could remember how to say was "Shut up and deal."

And try as he might, Melvinge couldn't remember when he had lost his ear. There was something in the back of his mind about an earring, and Melvinge thought that the earring might be important, or related somehow to the question of where the ear itself had gone, but every time he thought about it, he remembered less and less.

Frowning, Melvinge scratched his head instead of his ear, since he still had a head. That head—which we ought to describe before going on much further—was adorned with limp blond hair and covered with a beanie. The rest of Melvinge wore a striped shirt such as those favored by rugby players (for all that he'd never played rugby), dark blue shorts, and some kind of white footgear, rather grubby and dilapidated.

"The shoes mean something, I think," he mused. "But what?"

"Shut up and deal," said Rasputin.

Sure enough, the deck was sitting in front of Melvinge and all the other players were staring at him. He picked it up, gave the cards a quick riffle to add some more randomness to the universe, and started to deal.

But before he could lay down a single card, a blast of cold air raised the hair on the back of his neck. The door behind him opened, then slammed shut again. A tall, dark figure strode into the room, tilted a poke of dust on the bar, and called for drinks for the house. Then the stranger turned to look at all the Neitherworld card players.

Melvinge couldn't place the stranger's face, though he searched himself for a clue. The newcomer was dressed in a heavy topcoat over a blue pinstriped suit, with a silk scarf wrapped around his neck. The topcoat hung open, revealing a pair of M-79 grenade launchers in well-worn holsters on the stranger's hips. Then the man unwound the silk scarf and tucked it into a pocket.

A gasp ran around the room at the sight of the gill slits plainly visible on the stranger's neck.

"Uh-oh," Napoleon Bonaparte whispered to Alexander Graham Wiesnieuski, the telephone Pole. "Card Shark."

Sharks are Selachian fish, Melvinge remembered, the paragraphs of a long-ago biology text swimming up into the forefront of his memory. *They lack swim bladders, and their skeletons are cartilage rather than bone, but they're fish just the same.*

The stranger picked up his drink from the bar and plunked himself down at the card table directly across from Melvinge.

"Deal me in," he said.

Melvinge dealt.

The cards went around. The stranger turned out to be a lucky player—or maybe a little bit more than lucky. He had an unerring ability to pick the exact cards that he needed, and to keep the other players from making their pairs. As time went on, the game grew tenser and tenser—a change from sheer brain-rotting

34

tedium, it's true, but not one that Melvinge really appreciated.

Then the deal passed to the newcomer. The Card Shark's uncanny luck continued to hold.

"You're pretty good, stranger," Melvinge said.

The stranger picked a card. "Yeah."

"Mind if I ask you your name? Can't be calling you 'stranger' for an eternity or so."

"My name's Sdark."

The silence that followed spread out over the card room like a puddle of spilled motor oil. Everybody in the room seemed to know the name—it even rang a muffled and unpleasant chime in Melvinge's foggy memory.

"I thought Sdark was bigger than four Greyhound Buses end to end," Melvinge said finally, with an air of too-casual nonchalance.

The stranger didn't change expression. "Out in Time, Space, and the Other, maybe I am. Here's different."

Just how different Melvinge saw when he glanced down into the business end of an M-79.

"I'm Sdark," the stranger repeated. "And I'm looking for someone named Melvinge."

Melvinge swallowed. "You'll have to Go Fish."

"Nobody here by that name," a man from Piltdown contributed helpfully. "That's Vincent Van Gogh. You can tell by the ear."

"Shut up and deal," added Rasputin.

The muzzle of the M-79 didn't waver from Melvinge. "This next game is just between him and me," Sdark said.

The players looked from the Card Shark to Melvinge and then back at the Card Shark. Alexander the Great stood up, muttered something about having to go out and conquer Persia, and left. Rasputin followed, looking like a man with an urgent need to see a Czarina about a dog. One by one, the other players drifted out of the room.

Alone with Melvinge, Sdark the Card Shark shuffled, cut, and began to deal one-handed.

"What's the game?" Melvinge asked. At least, he thought, playing cards with Sdark would provide a change from the eternal rounds of Go Fish.

Sdark gave Melvinge a grin full of razor-edged, triangular teeth. "Blackjack."

Melvinge swallowed again. He didn't remember much about his life before the Neitherworld, but he felt pretty sure he'd never played anything more challenging than Old Maid with the deuces wild. "What are we going to bet?"

"Small stuff," Sdark said. "Something you never used. How about your soul?"

The first card fell in front of Melvinge. An ace. Then Sdark dealt himself a card. Another ace. Melvinge got his down card. When he peeked, he saw a third ace. Sdark dealt his own down card, and sat back to wait.

Melvinge sat with a pair of aces and wondered what to do. Aces could be worth either one or eleven, he remembered, as the rules for casino blackjack percolated up from the depths of his Neitherworld-fogged brain. So his hand was worth two, or twelve, or twenty-two.

Melvinge made his decision. He turned up his second card. "Split," he said.

Sdark dealt a fresh card faceup on top of each ace. The cards fell, a jack and a queen.

The face cards stirred up still more memories for Melvinge. The jack had a lop-eared, vaguely doglike appearance, and the queen held a painted fan before her dark, long-lashed gypsy eyes. *Harlan,* Melvinge thought. *And Loola.* Harlan had been his semifaithful dogoid companion back in Time, Space, and the Other, and Loola the Gypsy Princess had been his newly met (and now lost forever) dance partner and lady love.

"I stand," Melvinge said aloud. A pair of twenty-ones would be hard to beat.

Sdark turned up his down card—a deuce, leaving him with thirteen showing. The Card Shark dealt himself another card. A second deuce: fifteen. Then another card—a six.

"Twenty-one," Sdark said. "That's a push. A tie. Nothing done." He gathered the faceup cards to him, and placed them, still faceup, on the bottom of the deck.

"New deal," said the Card Shark. The M-79 remained pointed at Melvinge's face. "Your soul is still on the table."

Chapter 5

Dirty Work at the Gypsy Camp

Novaleen, she got the earring,
 Novaleen the Gypsy Queen,
Novaleen she cursed the earring,
 Ruthless Lady Novaleen.

—Blind Grapefruit

Meanwhile, over at the Gypsy encampment, a kettle was brewing that would render Melvinge's card game—and all the plans of his assorted friends for his eventual restoration to a mortal existence—decidedly Overcome by Events.

In the center of the ring of gaudily painted gypsy wagons, Novaleen the Gypsy Queen sat on a camp stool beside a glowing Coleman stove.[1] A battered and dented tin saucepan rested on the ring above the stove's blue flame. In the saucepan, a dark, unpleasant-looking glop seethed and bubbled. It smelled like a combination of melted rubber and formaldehyde.

A somewhat flea-bitten and entirely bald wolf lay on the tarmac by Novaleen's camp stool. He had his eyes closed and one paw held over his

[1]Just try getting a campfire going on bare concrete, without kindling. Even the most dedicated gypsy can't be blamed for taking whatever help she can get.

nose, in a futile attempt to shut out the worst of the smell from the simmering pot. A few feet away, an unshaven and unwashed individual stood making an equally futile attempt to clean the dirt out from under his fingernails with the point of a huge clasp knife.

From a hidden pocket in her multicolored and many-ruffled gypsy costume, Novaleen drew out a wallet-sized tri-vee photo with "Barsoom Bored of Trade Employment Office—Do Not Remove From Official File" stamped on the back. Novaleen's aged gypsy mother had given her the tri-vee on the morning of her twelfth birthday, intoning the mystic words as she did so, "Guard this well, O my daughter, 'cause someday you're gonna want it."

The tri-vee snapshot showed a middle-aged man with greasy blond hair and watery blue eyes. Novaleen held it out where both the wolf and the man could see it.

"Look carefully," she said. "Will you know him again?"

"Are you kidding?" said the man with the clasp knife. "That's Ratner. He's the bozo who hired me to get him the earring. He just left here—him and the dog and Loola."

"Don't get smart with me, Snake-Spit," said Novaleen. "I'm about to slap a full-strength curse on this Ratner person, and it's important to follow the script. You're going to have some work to do in a few minutes, so speak up. Will you know him?"

"Yeah, yeah, sure."

"Good," Novaleen told him. She looked down at the wolf. "What about you, Larry?"

The wolf opened his eyes for a second and squinted at the photograph. "Rrrrh-hrrrh," he said, and closed his eyes again. The steam rising from the bubbling pot was getting thicker and more malodorous by the minute.

"Excellent," said Novaleen, and dropped the trivee into the kettle. "All right, here we go. One curse, coming up."

As the photograph sank beneath the surface of the boiling glop, the Gypsy Queen began waving her hands back and forth above the kettle in a series of mystical gestures.

"O ye Spirits of the Megaverse," she chanted, "I hereby beseech ye to take in hand the one named Ratner, whose likeness I have thrown into the pot of sacred goulash in order that you might recognize him—for in truth, he is neither so good- nor so bad-looking that he would otherwise stand out in a crowd. Inflict upon him, I beseech ye, the Ancient Gypsy Curse of Amnesiac Finkhood. Let his nearest and dearest be as strangers to him, let his old acquaintances trust him not, nor yet be trusted by him in turn, and let all his kind thoughts and good intentions be warped into sinister motives and a generally bad attitude. And do not give me, O ye Spirits, any nonsense about whether or not Ratner deserves the treatment ye are about to lay upon him, for I have reasons of my own which are, pardon my saying so, none of your business. So I have spoken; so let it be done."

Novaleen lowered her hands to her lap and looked over at Snake-Spit. "That's the end of Part One. Do you have the earring?"

"Right here, said the freelance thug. He pulled the earring, and Melvinge's attached ear, out of his hip pocket. "You want it now?"

"Only for a moment," Novaleen told him. "Give it to me."

She took the earring and ear from Snake-Spit. The wolf eyed it, whining a little in his throat, for ears were his favorite food. "Down, Larry," she said.

Holding the rim of Melvinge's ear delicately between her thumb and forefinger, Novaleen dipped the earring into the kettle of glop. Clouds of green and yellow steam rose up, hissing, as the earring went under the surface, and the air was full of the odors of crankcase oil and battery acid.

"Phew!" exclaimed Snake-Spit. "What was *that*?"

"The Curse of Amnesiac Finkhood," Novaleen told him, "reacting with the metal and attaching itself to the earring. As soon as Ratner touches the earring the Curse will attach itself to him, instead. That's where you come in."

She pulled the earring and ear back up out of the accursed stew and held it out to Snake-Spit. The thug eyed the earring nervously and backed away.

"That thing ain't gonna hurt me, is it?"

"Snake-Spit," said Novaleen patiently, "how *could* it hurt you? You're already about as much

42

of a fink as it's possible for a humanoid to get. Now take this earring and go find Ratner."

Snake-Spit put his hands behind his back. "What's in it for me?"

"You can keep all the money," Novaleen promised him. "Or whatever else Ratner gives you, just as long as he gets the earring."

"What about that ear?" asked the thug. "You want me to take it off for you first?" He flicked his clasp knife suggestively.

"The ear stays," said Novaleen, as Larry looked at the ear and whimpered. "And you go. Now."

She held out the earring. After a few seconds of sulking, Snake-Spit took it (and the ear) and faded off into the shadowy depths of the Parking Lot. Novaleen turned to the wolf.

"All right, Larry. Give him a good head start and then you can follow him. Remember, all Ratner has to do is touch the earring. After that, I want the earring back—and I don't care how you get it."

Chapter 6

Revelations in the Riverfront Spamshop

I went down to the Riverfront Spamshop,
  Saw Melvinge there that day
Sitting down in front of a Card Shark,
  Well I looked, and I turned away.
                                    —Blind Grapefruit

In the Neitherworld, the game of blackjack between Melvinge and Sdark had gone on for a long time. Too long. Melvinge and the Card Shark had played forty-three straight hands, and had come to forty-three straight pushes. Enough of this sort of thing, and even playing for your immortal soul can get dull.

"Do you think there's such a thing as chance?" Melvinge asked. He looked at his cards. They added up to seventeen. "I'll stand."

"Has to be," Shdark replied. He turned up a thirteen, and drew a four. "I've got seventeen. That's another push."

He gathered the cards together, and threw a pasteboard face up in front of Melvinge. A king. It had Ratner's face this time. Again the card stirred up memories for Melvinge, but while he was certain that the grubby-looking man in the dirty apron was an important figure from his

45

past, he couldn't remember why.

Sdark dealt himself a two, then threw a card facedown in front of Melvinge and another one in front of himself. But this time Melvinge didn't bother to look at his down card. Instead he got to his feet.

Took me long enough to figure things out, he thought. *Sdark can't kill me if I'm already dead.*

"I'm sorry," he told the Card Shark. "This just isn't interesting."

He went to the bar and settled his tab without glancing back at where Sdark sat—still holding, Melvinge supposed, the M-79. Melvinge sauntered over to the door and flung it open. Only then did he turn to look back into the room.

"By the way," he said to the bartender, in a voice loud enough to reach the watching Card Shark, "my name *isn't* Vincent Van Gogh. It's Melvinge."

Then he walked out the door and closed it behind him.

Someone was waiting for him in the alley. It was the woman with the henna hair and the rhinestone sunglasses.

"I've been looking for you," she said. "What kept you?"

"Nothing important," Melvinge replied.

Just then, the card room door blew outward with the blast from a 40mm grenade—courtesy of Sdark's M-79.

"I think maybe we should be going," Melvinge said.

"Follow me," the woman said. "We need to talk."

The two headed down the alley, took a right on a cross street, and went down a block to a bus stop with movie posters advertising *The Doom That Came to Sarnoth*. Pretty soon a bus came by with a signboard announcing that it was the 15A bus (Kosmos and Aion—Terminus). Melvinge and the woman got on and took seats up front near the driver.

"Suppose you tell me what this is all about," Melvinge said. "Starting with who you are."

"I'm three hundred years old, and I come from the Bronx," the woman began. "My true name isn't even a word in your language, so you might as well call me Ruth. I'm also one of the Five Enlightened Masters, but that isn't important now. Ah, here's our stop."

She pulled the cord. The signal sounded like *Dies Irae* played on a banjo. The bus slowed, and the doors wheezed open.

"Your stop," called the driver. "Watch your step going out, please."

Melvinge followed the woman down to the sidewalk. She pointed to a nearby building. "We can talk in there."

Even more than the red letters painted on the front window, the peculiar odor of lard and dishwater told Melvinge that once again he stood in front of the Riverfront Spamshop.

"I was waiting in here for you when you first got to the Neitherworld," Ruth said, "but you didn't come inside. Then I almost picked you up at the rat races, but you got away. And once you hooked up with Sdark, I couldn't do anything until you left the game."

They entered the Spamshop and took seats at a table near a window overlooking the river. The eatery smelled even worse inside, reminding Melvinge of why he hadn't gone in there to start with.

"I'm not hungry, you know," he said to Ruth. "In fact, I haven't been hungry since I got here."

"No one is ever hungry in the Neitherworld," said Ruth. "That's what makes the restaurants here such ideal places to meet. Nobody ever goes into one for any reason. Complete privacy guaranteed."

Maybe, thought Melvinge, with a faint and un-Neitherworldly stirring of hope, *there really is something else to do around here besides play cards and watch rat races.*

"Okay," he said aloud, "we're private. What is it you've got to tell me?"

"I'll give it to you short and sweet," Ruth said. "You were on a Quest before you came here."

Melvinge nodded slowly. "Now that you've brought the subject up, I do seem to remember something like that."

"This is important," said Ruth. "Think. Can you remember what that Quest was?"

He shuffled his feet uneasily under the table. "I don't believe I . . . wait a minute. Feet. Shoes. The shoes are important. *I needed a new pair of shoes.*"

Melvinge stared at Ruth with a wild surmise. "I was trying to find the Megaverse Mall!" Then his face fell. "But that doesn't matter anymore, seeing as I'm dead."

"Dead, schmed," said Ruth. "Listen to me, young man. You are the only person who can find the Megaverse Mall. If you don't find it, no one else will ever find it."

"But I'm dead!" protested Melvinge.

"Details, details. First you have to get back to Time, Space, and the Other. Then you have to find the Mall."

"How do I do that?"

"Beats me," said Ruth. "You're the hero. You figure it out."

Melvinge sat back in his seat and looked at Ruth. He'd hoped for something to cheer up the Neitherworld's endless boredom—but while this latest bit of information hadn't been boring, he wouldn't exactly have called it cheerful. And he still didn't know what had happened to his missing ear.

In the next moment, the noise of the Spamshop's front door crashing open gave him something else to think about. Sdark the Card Shark stood there, his broad, pinstriped form blocking the entire doorway. He had his twin M-79s in his hands, and they were both pointed at Melvinge.

Chapter 7

Hitchhikers on the Interstate

Traveling down that Interstate,
  Listen to the timeskipper whine.
Farewell to reason and sweet common sense,
  I'm leaving you behind.

                 —Blind Grapefruit

    While Melvinge played cards with Sdark in the Neitherworld, and Melvinge's friends searched the vastness of the Parking Lot for the life-giving doors of the Megaverse Mall, Keester Button was sailing at high speed down the Interstate in a shiny pink and blue Spradillac, humming the *Agnus Dei* from Bach's B Minor Mass and keeping a sharp eye out for Plonkomatics.

    The geeky little fellow in the passenger seat hadn't said a word since they'd pulled out of Pinkie's. Now, all of a sudden, he started to jump up and down in his seat, pointing frantically to the side of the road.

    "What is it?" Keester snarled. "I don't see any Plonks over there."

    "Those guys, those two guys, pick 'em up," the geeky fellow said.

    "Okay," Keester said. "But if they try to dip into the guacamole, they're out of here."

Keester pulled off the Interstate, rolled down the breakup lane, put the Spradillac into reverse, and powered back. He pulled up in a flurry of dust beside two characters who stood by the side of the road. One of them had his thumb stuck out, and the other held up a hand-lettered sign reading "Mall."

"How far are you going, brother?" asked the nearer of the two, the one in the blue Hawaiian shirt with yellow palm trees and white orchids painted on it.

"Going as far as I have to," Keester said. "Jump in."

The two slid into the back seat. Keester powered away from the side of the road and back into the traffic stream.

"I'm Herk," said the guy in the flowered shirt.

"And I'm Bare," said his companion, who wore a tasteful café-au-lait birthday suit.

"I can see that," said Keester.

"No, I mean that's my name," said Bare.

"Right," said Keester, looking left and changing lanes to the center of the Interstate. "I'm Keester Button, and this little geeky fellow is—"

"Malfruddin."

That was the first time Keester had heard the name of his traveling companion. Had he been paying attention, he would have heard an ominous series of crashing minor chords played by a full orchestra on some other plane of existence, but Keester was sometimes unobservant.

"I couldn't help noticing that you guys were heading for the Mall," said Keester, who *was* able to pick up on some things. "Hope you aren't disappointed that I'm not heading there."

"But you are," said Herk, with a dazzling smile.

"Wrong answer, guy. I'm looking for my clone, and when I catch up with him, its going to be Resorbtion City, if you know what I mean."

"Your quest and ours are the same," said Bare, his smile equally dazzling. "When we reach the Mall, you shall find your clone, and all will be right with the worlds."

Keester frowned. "Worlds?"

"Indubitably," replied Herk.

"What makes you think so?"

Herk and Bare exchanged glances. "Have a glance," said Herk.

"Thank you," said Bare. "Have one of mine."

That little ritual concluded, Herk explained.

"You may think us crazy," he began.

"Mad, loopy," Bare interjected.

"But we have learned, through concentrated study of certain ancient manuscripts, that someone, someday, will find the way to the Mall."

"Oh, come on," Keester said. "People find the Mall all the time. Finding the way there is the easiest thing there ever was. Look."

He pointed out the front window of the Spradillac. A white-on-green highway sign proclaimed Megaverse Mall, Next 200 Exits.

"None of them believe," Bare said, shaking his head.

"Ask yourself this," Herk said. "Have you ever been to the Mall?"

53

"Well, no," Keester admitted.

Herk pressed on. "Do you know anyone who's ever been to the Mall?"

Keester shook his head. "No."

"Does anyone you know, know anyone who's been to the Mall?"

"No," said Keester. A thought occurred to him. "But that's not too surprising. I mean, I was only cloned about two months ago, and I've met, counting you guys, maybe half a dozen people, tops."

"They always have a reason," Bare commented sadly. "And it always sounds so reasonable."

"*I* believe you," said Malfruddin to the two in the back seat. "Tell me what you've learned."

"We are traveling," said Herk, "with a Purpose. For we have discovered in the course of our studies—studies that from their very nature required wide, and at the same time minutc, research and the consultation of works of a very recondite character—and taking into account not only the very limited extent of our own libraries, but the distance of our abodes from any of the great libraries of the land, where rare and expensive works may be consulted, the due course of our work was attended by many difficulties—"

"The kindness of strangers, however," Bare cut in, "has tended wonderfully to remove these difficulties."

"Yes, but what did you *learn*?" Malfruddin asked, a strange gleam coming to his eyes.

"You have heard, perhaps, of the Hero with a Single Ear?" Herk asked.

"Er, no," said Keester. "Should I have?"

"That will make the explanation a bit more difficult," said Bare. "But not too difficult."

"Yes, yes," said Malfruddin impatiently. "Tell me what you've learned."

"Um, is that guacamole dip?" Herk asked, pointing to the bowl on the front seat between Keester and Malfruddin. "It has been some days since we both have eaten."

"Tell us your secret," Keester said. "Then you can eat."

Herk sat back, and crossed his arms. "I do not believe, Bare, that these gentlemen desire enlightenment," he said.

"Hardly," Bare agreed, also settling back.

Malfruddin and Keester exchanged glances. (By now, not one single glance was still with its original owner.) "It's important," Malfruddin whispered. "Remember, they said that your clone would be at the Mall? They know something. Come on, it's only mashed avocados."

"All right," Keester growled between his teeth. "Take the dip. But this secret had better be pretty darned secret, to make it worth a whole bowl."

"Oh, it is," said Herk, suddenly cheerful as he snatched the bowl of dip. Bare pulled a bag of turnip chips from his duffle bag, and shared them out with Herk. The two hitchhikers began to snack in the back seat, trying not to get too many blobs of dip on the upholstery, for guacamole stains horribly if it isn't cleaned up right away.

"Now the secret," Keester said, when Herk and

55

Bare had reduced the chips and dip to crumbs and scrapings.

"Oh, that," said Bare. "Yes. The secret is that there is one man, a Hero, who can find the way to the Mall."

"And he will have a shrine in the Parking Lot," said Herk.

"Finding the shrine will be easier than finding the Mall," Bare added. "There's just one problem."

"What's that?" Malfruddin wanted to know.

"The Hero's dead," Bare told him. "He died before he could find the Mall."

"Don't forget," said Herk to his companion. "Unless the Sethians, the Naasenians, and the Orphites are all wrong—and I refuse to even admit the possibility—there's also a reptile involved in this somehow."

"What it comes down to, of course," Bare commented after a moment of silence, "is that this Hero isn't as dead as he looks. He can still lead us to the Mall. He's our only chance of getting there, in fact."

"Can you tell me one thing that will convince me that you two aren't total nutcases?" Keester wanted to know.

"Nothing that comes instantly to mind," admitted Herk.

"I'm going to throw you two out of the car right now," Keester said. "I might slow down first, but I doubt it."

Keester put the Spradillac on autopilot, and started clambering into the rear seat.

"If you throw us out, you'll never find the Mall," warned Bare.

"That doesn't worry me," Keester said, as he pushed the button that popped the explosive bolts holding on the back door. "I'm not looking for the Mall, remember?"

"You're looking for a Plonkomatic," said Herk. "It was driven by a fleshopod like yourself, but his name is Sid."

"It's parked in the Parking Lot of the Megaverse Mall," said Bare. "But Sid isn't with the Plonk anymore."

Keester stopped. "I didn't mention any of this stuff," he said, baffled. "How do you know who I'm looking for and what he's driving?"

"It is written," said Herk, brushing turnip-chip crumbs off his shirt. "Now if you will stop and let us off, since I can see that you do not desire the benefits of our erudition—"

"No, no, not at all," said Keester, climbing back into the driver's seat. "Please stay. I want to learn more."

"Very well," said Bare. "The exit you want is coming up. We'll tell you when."

Chapter 8

Lounge Lizards and Other Reptiles

Ratner, Ratner was standing near,
When in loped Larry eyeing Melvinge's ear.
"Ratner, Ratner, I see what you got,
It's gonna be mine in the Parking Lot."
                              —Blind Grapefruit

In the Parking Lot of the Megaverse Mall, Ratner had been tramping for an hour or so between the endless lines of empty cars. Then out of the dark (for the helium vapor lamps in this part of the lot had gone out some time before and had never been replaced), a voice hissed from behind a tour bus, "Hey, Ratner, over here!"

Ratner looked to his right. Something dark and man-shaped was moving in the shadows.

"Who's there?" he called out.

"UPS," came the answer. "Untied Package Schleppers. I got something here for you."

"Great!" Ratner took a step in the direction of the shadows. Under normal circumstances, he might have been a little more suspicious, since Untied Package didn't make deliveries to the Parking Lot—but circumstances, as we shall see, were not normal. "Give it to me."

"Not so fast, snark-breath. You owe me."

Ratner halted. "Didn't you get paid already?"

"Uh . . . yeah. I got expenses, though."

"Expenses? How much?"

"Five bucks, plus six percent sales tax, comes to five thirty."

"Oh, okay." Ratner dug in his pockets, and came up with five singles and two quarters. "Got change?"

"I'll owe it to ya."

Ratner pulled back his hand, and the money with it. "What kind of gyp is this?"

"You want the delivery or not?"

"Oh, okay, I won't quibble over twenty cents." Ratner handed over the money. In return, the shadowy figure handed back an earring, with the ear still attached.

"Here you go, sport," said Snake-Spit, the free-lance thug—for of course, the mysterious shadowy figure was actually none other than our ear-stealing friend. "Wear it in good health." He laughed and then faded, still laughing, back into the shadows.

Ratner paid no attention to Snake-Spit's departure or to the odor of crankcase oil and battery acid that seemed to waft by as his fingers brushed the earring. He was too busy turning the ear over and over in his hands. *Mine at last,* he thought. *The Earring of Erk is mine, and there's no way Harlan can suspect that I'm the one who got it!*

The ear attached to the earring was something else. *I wonder who sent this to me. My birthday isn't until next August, and I don't remember asking anyone for an ear.*[1]

He tried to work the fastener on the back of the earring. It didn't want to come loose from Melvinge's ear.

"Oh, well," Ratner said. Maybe when it got light he would be able to figure it out. But right then he had to keep track of the earring somehow.

After a moment's thought he clipped the ring to his own earlobe—something the clasp seemed willing to allow, as long as the earring still had Melvinge's ear hanging from it. The overall effect was rather charming, in a punkish kind of way.

With the earring, and ear, safely fixed in place, Ratner took a sight on O'Brien, the third star from the right in the constellation Cheeseburger (nearly due south at that time of year), and turned back to seeking the Mall.

Ratner, however, was not as alone as he thought he was. True, the raucous music of the gypsy camp had faded with distance, but one member of the gypsy band was far closer. The whole time Ratner and Snake-Spit had been talking, Larry Halibut—part-time novelist and

---

[1]There are a lot of things, right now, that Ratner isn't remembering. What he's got—in addition to the infamous Gypsy Curse of Amnesiac Finkhood, already hard at work stripping his little grey cells of memory after memory—is the fabled Earring of Erk, which all on its own will make the one who wears it devious and clever, and will cause reality to shift and change unexpectedly around him. The combination of curse and earring is not one that bodes well for Ratner—or for anyone else.

61

full-time werewolf—had been crouched in the shadows on top of the tour bus, where he could see and hear everything.

"That earring belongs to Novaleen," Larry muttered. Such asides were a habit that he'd picked up while writing *Everybody in Heck*, book ten in the twelve-volume *Norbert Spinoff's Plagueyears* series. He had found mumbling aloud on the part of otherwise minor characters a useful way to get in the necessary exposition. As a result, he now spent a great deal of time talking to himself.

Larry eyed the earring, and both of the ears attached to it. While he was at it, he also eyed the matching ear on the other side of Ratner's head. If Larry had a weakness (other than muttering important things so that the people around him would know them too), it was a fondness for goulash made of human ears. Call it part of being a werewolf. Also, like wolves everywhere, this particular wolf was very loyal to the pack leader—and for better or worse, Novaleen the Gypsy Queen was the leader of Larry's particular pack.

Larry gathered himself to spring. But Ratner made off southward before the werewolf could leap, and Larry sank back onto his haunches.

"What the heck," Larry muttered. Since the moon wasn't full, he wasn't in complete wolf shape and didn't have a complete set of fangs anyway. "A brisk stalk through the Parking Lot will do me good."

Silently, the werewolf dropped to the tarmac and followed Ratner as the former short-order cook made his way to the south.

*   *   *

Meanwhile, not far off to the west, the dancer Loola had paused in the light cast by a circle of torches.

The folks in this camp were not gypsies, but rather a roving band of Motorcycle Monks. Some time before, when they had first arrived in the Parking Lot of the Megaverse Mall, the Motorcycle Monks had parked their chopped hogs in a circle. At nightfall on that first day, they had tied flaming pine knots to the handlebars of their motorcycles to illuminate their camp—a custom they still followed each evening as darkness fell.

They had been in the same location for three years now, and had constructed semipermanent booths and lean-tos around their motorcycles. In these crude buildings the monks worked at making trinkets of carved jade, which they traded to passersby for information about the true direction of the Megaverse Mall.

The monks' jade had come from the Jaded Outlook, a spur of rock on their homeworld overlooking the Slough of Despond and the Pit of the Stomach. After three years their supplies of jade had started to run low, giving a new urgency to their quest for the One True Mall (where, of course, gem and mineral shops abound, and where jade of all colors from deepest green to pure milk white can be bought for a song. The monks had a number of songs all racked up and ready for bartering when the great day of discovery should at last arrive).

None of this historical information would have

been of interest to Loola—who was, in fact, moving rather sluggishly. By now the sun was below the horizon, and Loola didn't care about the Mall anymore. She just wanted to find someplace warm where she could rest until she had recovered her strength.

This had been (to put it mildly) an exciting day. First she had met the man who'd won her heart with a single glance, only to see him shot down like a dog on the highway. Then, before she'd even had a chance to think things over, a genuine dog on the highway had talked her into going off alone in search of the Megaverse Mall. It was all hardly to be believed, and Loola felt quite faint.

She staggered into the motorcyclists' camp, and leaned against the side of one of their shanties. The sheet of corrugated iron was still warm from the sun, and Loola felt instantly better as she rested against it. As she stood there, a man wearing a saffron-yellow leather jacket approached her. He pulled off his pale-green stone motorcycle helmet, revealing a shaven head.

"Ah, young woman, welcome to our simple camp," the man said. "You do us honor with your presence."

"I'm only resting here a while," Loola said. "I have a long way to go."

"Longer than you think, perhaps," the man said, "but not so long as you fear. Permit me to introduce myself. I am Brother Ojibway Khartoum, a humble seeker after knowledge."

"My name is Loola," she said. "Loola Siisdaughter." She fanned herself with her little gypsy fan. "Say, are you related to Ojibway ben Coyote, the Jet Eye Night?"

"No," Ojibway said. "I do not do windows, nor do I do media parodies. The Farce has too strong a power over the weak minded." His face grew so stern that Loola became frightened.

"But tell me," Brother Ojibway continued in a softer tone after a moment had passed, "what is your quest?"

"I'm looking for the Megaverse Mall," Loola replied. "Do you know where it is?"

He shook his head. "That, I confess, is the very knowledge that I am humbly seeking. You came from the east; does the Mall lie in that direction?"

"No," she said. "At least, it doesn't lie a hundred yards in that direction, which is how far I've come."

"But you came here with a secret," Ojibway said.

Loola looked at him nervously. The stored warmth of the corrugated iron no longer cheered her.

For Ojibway Khartoum had spoken the truth, gained in who-knew-what obscure manner. Loola's inner secret, one never revealed even to friends, acquaintances, lovers, or family members, was that she was really a lizard. Cold reptilian blood coursed through her veins, and tended to slow her down after dusk, especially when the air got chilly. Makeup covered the scales, and long ruffled skirts over layers of lacy petticoats concealed her tail and her decidedly odd legs. To aid in the disguise, she carried a fan, and waved it in front of her face whenever she felt the absolute need to flick her little pink forked tongue.

She waved it now. "I have to be going," she said.

"I think you should stay, for a little while at least," Ojibway said. "Your secret is safe with me. There are other seekers here, and perhaps a way for you to gain enlightenment."

He led the way across the circle of parked motorcycles, each with its pair of blazing torches, to an area where round tables covered with red-checked tablecloths surrounded a cleared area. A group of Thecodonts sat at one of the tables, whispering together.

"Two nights ago, these creatures came from the west," Ojibway said. "They spoke of dancing. There is a dance contest, it seems, one that is to be held a week from tonight in the Parking Lot that faces the Gondwana interchange."

"What's that to me?" Loola asked.

"This is merely a local contest, it is true," Ojibway said. "But it is said that the winner of each local contest goes on to the regionals, the winners of the regionals go on to the nationals, and so on."

"I still don't see what that has to do with me."

Ojibway Khartoum smiled wisely. "The finals, it is said, are held in the Mall itself."

"Ah," said Loola. "Now I understand." She felt gypsy pride running hot in her otherwise cold blood—for what gypsy, even if she is really a lizard, cannot outdance a whole floorful of ordinary mortals? "Even if I can't find the Mall, if I win the dance contests I can make the Mall find me."

"Precisely," said Ojibway Khartoum.

Then Loola's face fell, as she remembered her only-recently-discovered and even-more-recently-deceased True Love, the unfortunate Melvinge. With him, she felt sure, she could have danced as no gypsy had ever danced before. Without him . . .

"I'm sorry," Loola said. "I can't. Not without my Own True Love. My heart just wouldn't be in it."

"Then fetch him," Ojibway said, with a wave of his hand, "and you will both dance."

"I can't," said Loola. "He's dead."

"But *I'm* not," came a voice from the shadows. A man stepped forward into the torchlight. It was Snake-Spit, the freelance thug. "You can dance with me, sweet thing. We'll make it to the Mall together."

Chapter 9

Strange Companions and
Other Odd Fellows

Some of these days and it won't be long,
  Sid is going to find the Mall.
You'll look for him and he'll be gone,
  Sid is going to find the Mall.

—Blind Grapefruit

It was late afternoon in the Parking Lot of the Megaverse Mall. Sid the amorphoid fleshopod looked out the window of his Plonkomatic, still resting between the Studebaker and the dubious-looking Gypsy encampment. In the traffic lane between the rows of parked vehicles, a giant Galapagos tortoise trudged slowly by, the slogan "Mall or Bust!" painted on its massive shell in hot pink fingernail polish.

Sid watched the gaudily decorated tortoise from the windows of his Plonkomatic until the creature vanished over the horizon to the north. By then the sun was setting, and Sid tried to ignore the wild bursts of music and laughter from the gypsy camp. He had pretty good success. He even had fair success with the wild burst of gunfire that erupted when the sun was all the way down.[1] But he had no success at all, somewhere around midnight, with the sound of someone knocking at the driver's-side window of his stolen car.

He looked out the window and saw a nattily dressed dog with the limp body of a man slung over one shoulder. Against his better judgment, Sid rolled down the window.

"What do you want?" he asked.

"I need a hand carrying my boss, here," the dog replied. "I hadn't realized how heavy he is, and I'd sure hate to leave him behind."

Sid stared, amazed. It wasn't possible, but there they were—the same pair who had shown up at Pinkie's just that morning, looking for kumquat shakes. The multiverse didn't have so many well-dressed dogs teamed up with beanie-wearing nebbishes that Sid could be making a mistake.

Maybe the dog doesn't recognize me, Sid thought. *After all, amorphoid fleshopods all look pretty much the same to anyone who isn't a fleshopod. Or maybe he's working for Sdark. Better play along, just in case.*

"Sure, I'll help you," Sid said.

He got out of the Plonkomatic, and was about to lock up when he made a fast decision.

Easy come, easy go, he thought, and left the keys in the ignition, with the pseudobrain in neutral and the door unlocked. *Maybe the next thing to come along will need a car as badly as I needed one this morning.*

---

[1]The sound, of course, of Larry the Gypsy Werewolf hard at work doing in our hero Melvinge with a silver bullet.

He stood by the side of the Plonkomatic, stretched, and extruded a pair of pseudopods from his back. "Hook him up there," Sid said, and stooped over so that Harlan could drape Melvinge's corpse more conveniently onto the makeshift rack.

"Where to now?" Sid asked, when the faithful hound had boosted Melvinge onto the pseudopods.

"We're heading east," Harlan replied. "I gotta get my boss to the Resurrections B Us franchise at the Megaverse Mall."

Chapter 10

On the Road to the Really Big Dance Hall

There ain't nothing at all, down at the Mall,
'Cept a Parking Lot, and when folks call,
They're dancin' nightly in the Hall.
—Blind Grapefruit

A few generalized megaversal timeperiods[1] after the fateful events at the Gypsy encampment, Keester Button guided the Spradillac containing Herk, Bare, Malfruddin, and himself off the Interstate at the Gondwana interchange after paying a purely nominal toll.

The unlikely quartet cruised for a long while through the lanes of the Parking Lot before pulling up behind a Mini Super that seemed quite abandoned. A fading poster reading Big Dance Contest Tonite! Parking Lot Section Green Three. Prizes! Spiritual Advancement! was plastered across one side of the little vehicle, and a woodchuck had made its den in the back seat. After checking both ways, the four travelers piled out of the Spradillac, picked up the Mini, moved it out into the traffic lane, and took its parking space for themselves.

[1]A year, a month, a week, a natural day . . . time has a way of getting elastic in the Parking Lots of the Megaverse Mall.

king in the direction of the
figure. The humanoid figure
an old man sitting on the
dark glasses on his face and
at in front of him. A couple of
a zloty or two lay in the hat, but
ould live on. The man wore a sign
a loop of string around his neck: God
Bless You, You Can See! Help the Grapefruit Man.
He was singing a slow blues song about someone
called Melvinge.

"Hey, guy, which way to the Mall?" Keester
asked.

The blind man kept on singing.

"Does anyone know where this Mall is?" Malfruddin demanded.

Blind Grapefruit (for this was, of course, the
Blind Bard of the Megaverse himself, the only
being in any reality who understands everything)
began a long riff on the blues harp.

"This man cannot help us," Herk said in a pious
tone.

"It is clear he knows nothing," Bare agreed,
nodding. The four travelers trudged off north-
ward, and the Parking Lot minstrel continued
his song behind them.

They traveled on for some time without seeing any structure that resembled the Megaverse
Mall. Keester Button was starting to growl under
his breath. Herk and Bare, however, remained
as cheerful as ever. So, unaccountably, did Malfruddin.

The sun was straight up overhead when they

encountered the man with the earring. It was a most unusual earring—since besides the usual gems, precious metals, cowrie shells, and raspberry Life Savers, it was ornamented with a dangling, severed ear. The man himself, however, had no distinguishing characteristics to speak of, except for a faint odor of battery acid and crankcase oil about his grease-stained apron and fleeting traces of devious cleverness in his watery blue eyes.

"Hey, you," said Keester Button to the guy with the earring. "Which way is the Mall?"

"I'm a stranger here myself," said the man. "There's a big building up ahead, though, and I'm heading that way."

He pointed, and the four travelers saw that a huge structure did indeed loom up above the rooftops of the parked cars. They all hurried onward.

But as they came nearer, it became plain that this was not the Megaverse Mall after all—not unless the Megaverse Mall was constructed entirely of old cars and Pepsi cans. The gaping door glittered in the morning sunshine with the shards of broken tail reflectors. Over the door, in headlights (unilluminated at the moment), a name was spelled out: Really Big Dance Hall.

Just then Malfruddin pointed at a vehicle parked in the very shadow of the Dance Hall. "Hey, that's my Plonkomatic! I'd know it anywhere."

"Then my clone has to be somewhere around here," Keester growled.

Someone stepped out of a sunny spot just inside

the door: a filthy and unshaven thug holding a large clasp knife and wearing a T-shirt with the motto Mammon Slept Here emblazoned on the front.

"You guys want to dance with a lady?" he asked, his tone implying that he already knew the answer. "Cost ya a dime."

Before they could answer, a young woman in gypsy costume came out of the dance hall. She approached the travelers with a smooth, gliding step, her long ruffled skirts rustling over the tarmac as she passed.

"Take a hike, Snake-Spit," she said to the thug with the clasp knife. "This one's a friend." She looked at the man with the earring over the top of her little gypsy fan.

"Hey there, Ratner," she said. "How about a dance? For you, it's free."

"Loola!" said Ratner—for the gypsy lizard was neither near enough nor dear enough to him for coverage under the Gypsy Curse of Amnesiac Finkhood.[2] "How did you get here?"

She gave a graceful shrug. "I came with some friends of mine. We found a Plonkomatic somebody had left in the Parking Lot with its pseudobrain in neutral. The door was unlocked, and the keys were in the ignition, so we drove it on over here and entered the local Dance Contest. Everybody says that the national finalists are going to dance at the Megaverse Mall."

"Who won the locals?" asked Ratner.

[2]She didn't care all that much about him, either, as far as that goes.

76

"I did, of course," said Loola. "The regional semi-finals are tomorrow, and I'll win them, too—if I decide to dance, that is."

"Of course you will dance," said Malfruddin. Here in the shadow of the Really Big Dance Hall, his voice had grown considerably stronger, and his presence had become suspiciously forceful for a character with geeky eyebrows.

"I am a Gypsy," said Loola. "I dance when I please." She looked at him over the edge of her fan for a moment, before disappearing back inside the hall in a rustle of ruffled skirts.

Herk and Bare looked at each other. "Does she understand the truth, brother?" Herk asked his companion.

"She has not studied the ancient texts, as we have," said Bare. "And she does not look like someone to whom a revelation has been granted."

"But she does, perhaps, have an inkling," Herk said. "After all, she is selling dances, and selling is what the Mall is all about."

"Indeed," said Bare. "She may be one of those who are ready to understand the truth when it is properly explained. As, of course, we are prepared to do."

Malfruddin turned his gaze upon the two wandering mystics. "Why don't you guys explain it to *me*, first?"

"Gladly," Bare said. He turned to his companion. "Should we give it to them simply, and dispense with the proofs?"

"I think so, really," said Herk. "If these fine folks are willing to believe, then they should do so without proof, since without study they won't understand the proof anyway."

"So what *is* the secret?" demanded Keester Button.

"Why, that there is no Mall," Herk said.

"No Mall!" exclaimed Ratner. The earring and its pendant ear bobbed vigorously from the strength of his reaction. Keester Button frowned. Malfruddin continued to regard the two visionaries with a thoughtful expression.

"At least, there is no Mall in the usual way in which things are said to exist," Bare amended.

"It's like this," continued Herk. "What is a chair?"

"I'm about to become violent," Keester said in a pleasant, conversational voice.

"No, really, how can you tell that a thing is a chair?" asked Herk, not seeming to expect a reply. "When you come to an object, right away, without having to ask anyone, you know whether it's a chair or not. It isn't the material, you know. Some chairs are made of wood and others are metal . . ."

"Don't forget the fabric-covered ones," Bare added.

"Definitely not," said Herk. "In the same way, it isn't the number of legs, either, since some chairs have four legs, and some only have one."

"Some don't have legs at all," said Bare. "Look at beanbag chairs, if you will."

"But still," Herk said, "all of them are chairs."

"What's all this stuff about chairs have to do with the Megaverse Mall?" asked Ratner.

"I'm getting to that," said Herk. "The reason that you know these things are chairs is that there exists an Ideal Chair. As objects do and do not resemble the Ideal Chair, so you say they are and are not chairs."

"It is clear," Bare went on, "that the Ideal Chair is closer to being a Barcalounger than it is to being a folding metal chair, but still that folding chair partakes of chairness, wouldn't you agree?"

"Undoubtedly," said Herk. "When we have a four-legged chair, and one of the legs is shorter than the others, so that the chair wobbles, that does not stop it from being a chair, but nevertheless we say that it is an evil chair, since it falls short of being a perfect chair by that certain degree."

"Doesn't this imply that a spindle-back chair is more evil than a Laz-E-Boy?" Bare asked.

"Not at all, not at all," said Herk. "Merely that it is less good."

"Wait a minute, wait a minute," said Ratner. "What are you telling us about the Mall?"

"Why, that it sells Ideal Chairs," said Herk. "It must, being an Ideal Mall. But as I was saying—just as you recognize a chair by how close it comes to being an Ideal Chair, so you will recognize that a thing is red by how closely it partakes of Ideal Redness, and you recognize the Good by how close it comes to Ideal Goodness."

"And just where *are* all these ideals?" Malfruddin asked.

"At the Ideal Mall, of course," said Bare.

"And where is the Mall?" By now, a more

practical man than either of our two vision-
ary friends would have taken warning from the
entirely ungeeky look in Malfruddin's eyes, and
cut short the explanation—but Herk and Bare
were not the sort to resist the missionary urge.

"We carry the Mall within ourselves," Herk told
him. "The word *ideal* comes from the word *idea,*
and that means the Ideal Mall is a figment of our
imaginations."

"I have in *my* mind an Ideal Beating," inter-
rupted Keester Button, "and I am about to admin-
ister it to you two if you don't shut up. There is
only One Mall, and only . . . and only . . . ' "

" 'And only Malfruddin knows where it is,' "
Malfruddin supplied for him. "Isn't that right,
Ratner?"

Ratner blinked hard once or twice, as the Earring of Erk tried its best to supply him with
enough wiliness and all-around smarts to resist
the combined whammy of Amnesiac Finkhood and
Malfruddin's forceful personality. Then the odor of
crankcase oil and battery acid intensified, and the
earring gave up its efforts in disgust.

"That's right," Ratner said. "We shall go
throughout the Parking Lot to bring customers
to the Really Big Dance Hall, where they will
dance to Malfruddin's music and discover from
him the One True Way to the Megaverse Mall."

Once again, Herk and Bare looked at each other. "I believe, brother," said Herk sadly, "that it
is time for us to go elsewhere."

Chapter 11

Strange Encounters in the Neitherworld and Elsewhere

While Melvinge sat in the Neitherworld
  He had no luck at all,
But Harlan stood on the mountaintop
  And thought he saw the Mall.
                    —Blind Grapefruit

Sdark the Card Shark stalked into the Riverfront Spamshop.

"Why, Etaonrish, you old demiurge," he said to Ruth. "I should have known I'd find you here."

"Forget it, Sdark," said the lady with the hennared hair and the rhinestone sunglasses. "This guy doesn't have anything you want."

Sdark grinned his underslung, saw-toothed grin. Back in Time, Space, and the Other, Sdark had been a Loan Shark, and truly monumental in size. Here in the Neitherworld, however, he preferred to take on the shape of a large, sharp-toothed individual with gill slits showing above the collar of his blue pinstriped suit.

"Correction—he *does* have something I want," said Sdark. He turned to Melvinge, and the grin turned to a vicious snarl. "You humiliated me, you fool, back there in Time, Space, and the Other.

Nobody gets away from a Loan Shark and lives to tell the tale. I'm going to torture you from now until the end of time, and then fifteen minutes more just for good measure."

The Card Shark slid out a chair and plopped heavily into it, still pointing his M-79s at Melvinge and Ruth.

"He's already dead, you know," Ruth said to Sdark. "You can't really hurt him."

"Oh, yeah?" said Sdark. "Watch this."

The Card Shark gestured with one hand. The muzzle of that hand's M-79 described a complex pattern in the Spamshop air. Melvinge felt as if the top of his head was being pulled through the soles of his feet and vice versa, rather like a strip of saltwater taffy in a taffy-stretching machine.

"That's just the crude stuff," Sdark said. "I can get fancy. And if I get bored, maybe I will."

With the small corner of his mind Melvinge still had to think with, he groaned. From what he'd seen so far of the Neitherworld, Sdark was certain to get bored. Getting bored was the only thing to do around here. But there was one good thing about supreme torture, Melvinge decided: at least it would be a change from playing cards.

At the same moment that Melvinge was beginning his ultimate torture—although the word *same* doesn't mean very much when you're talking about the relationship between the Neitherworld and Time, Space, and the Other—the sun was rising over the Parking Lot of the Megaverse Mall. In the shadow on the west side of a beached and deserted ark, a pair of travelers paused to take their bearings.

"Give me a hand," said Harlan the dogoid to Sid the amorphoid fleshopod—for the two travelers were, in fact, none other than our friends, several months of hard questing further down the road to the Megaverse Mall. "I want to climb up and see where we are."

The ark lay tilted on its keel, filling several parking spaces and partly blocking a fire lane. It was easily three hundred cubits long by fifty cubits wide, and at least thirty cubits high. At one point, the sides of the antique vessel had been covered with reeds and smeared with pitch, but most of the reeds had fallen off, revealing the cypress ribs within.

Sid formed a stirrup with his upper, or handoid, pseudopods, and boosted Harlan toward the bottom sill of the door cut in the ark's side. Harlan grabbed the edge, and hauled himself through the opening. Then he reached down and pulled in Melvinge's body. Last of all, he gave Sid a hand up, so that all three were standing—rather stiffly, in Melvinge's case—on the tilted lower deck of the huge boat.

With Harlan leading the way, the travelers climbed from deck to deck, past empty stalls and cages. One cage, labeled *Daphoenus demilo,* still had its door closed. Dry bones inside the cage revealed the fate of the pair of animals who had once been imprisoned there.

At last they reached the main deck. From that

vantage point, Harlan looked out over the Parking Lot. Cars, nothing but cars. No Mall in sight in any direction. The ark's passenger cabin was nearby, and Harlan clambered up onto the cabin roof to give himself more range. Still no Mall.

He pulled Melvinge's corpse up onto the roof with him, and balanced it upright. Carefully, he climbed up onto his late boss's shoulders, and thus gained another five feet or so of elevation. Harlan looked all around, and saw nothing to the north, south, or west. But off to the east . . . could that be a shadow he saw along the horizon, like mountains viewed from a long distance, so far away that you can't tell if they're solid things or clouds?

"Sid, my friend," Harlan whispered, "I think we may have found something."

"Where?" Sid asked, jumping up and down, trying to see.

"Off east," Harlan said. "I think—I think I may have seen the Mall."

He pushed Melvinge's body off the roof of the cabin to the pavement below, and then jumped from the ark himself, using his boss's inert form to cushion the impact. After Sid had joined him, and had once more taken up Melvinge's body onto his dorsal pseudopods, the three began walking east again, this time with more spring in their steps (except for Melvinge, of course, who had no spring in his step at all).

They hiked all day, pausing only to consume a snack of Lizard-on-a-Stick at a seedy dive catering to people in search of the Mall entrance. When night fell, Harlan stood Melvinge upright and threw a tarp over him. As was his usual practice, Harlan then tied guylines from the tarp to the door handles of cars parked nearby. Under the shelter of this improvised tent, the dog and the fleshopod rested.

Harlan reached over to the car nearest him and sliced off a few pieces of tire. He arranged them in a pile, lit them, and settled down to make a pot of hot chocolate.

That night a cold rain started falling, and continued for three days. During the rainy spell, Harlan didn't break camp and kept the fire going by sending Sid out from time to time after more tires.

The cars in this part of the Parking Lot were older and looked as if they had been parked there longer than in some of the other areas Sid and Harlan had passed through. Many of the cars had long since lost all their tires to other campfires, and the paint from their bodies had rusted away. Drifts of dust—now mud, in the chilly rain—formed little mounds in between the empty vehicles.

If not for the shadow Harlan had glimpsed on the horizon, the dogoid would have been ready to call his quest a failure, and turn back to see what luck the others had enjoyed. Now, however, he expected to be at the Mall itself within a week, if only this dratted rain would stop.

He didn't want to take Melvinge's body out in the rain if he didn't have to. During the several months he had wandered since parting from

Loola and Ratner, the corpse had been left out in the weather a couple of times, and Melvinge was starting to show the wear. Of course, using him as a temporary article of furniture whenever Harlan happened to need something (a door, a couch, a footstool, an anchor) and mislaying him entirely once or twice hadn't helped. But now, with the goal of the Quest in sight, Harlan wasn't taking any chances.

So he was sitting under his tent on the third night, toasting marshmallows on a stick over a merrily crackling tire, when two strangers approached his camp.

"Say, brother, have you been saved?" one of them asked, as soon as the two came within speaking range.

"Our studies indicate that, in accordance with ancient doctrine, the end is near," said the other, "and can only be propitiated by a proper sacrifice."

"Sacrificing a marshmallow or two to a hungry prophet is just about right," said the first stranger, a man dressed in a gaudy Hawaiian shirt. "Allow us to introduce ourselves. I am Herk. And my partner, as you can see, is Bare."

Chapter 12

We Return to Our Epic Already in Progress

"Harlan, oh Harlan, what you got in your grip?"
"Piece of Melvinge's shoulder,
  Going to give him a trip."

—Blind Grapefruit

"The way it is," Herk said to Harlan several marshmallows later, as the two wandering prophets conversed with the dogoid and the amorphoid fleshopod in the little tent beside the mud puddle, "there is a True Mall, but it only exists in the mind."

" 'What mind?' you may ask," Bare interjected. "That is the point where all the ancient philosophers balk. But not us. We boldly go where angels with Masters' Degrees in Comparative Theology fear to tread. There is *one* mind . . ."

"A real mind, not a pseudomind. That's very important," Herk threw in.

" . . . *one* mind where the Ideal Mall is real, and that mind is the mind of a hero."

"Not just any hero," Herk added, "but a dead hero."

"Do you have any idea who this dead hero might be?" Harlan asked, leaning back against

Melvinge's corpse where it supported the tent. He struck a match on the sole of Melvinge's foot and lit a cigar. The fumes helped keep back the mosquitoes which rose in clouds over this part of the Parking Lot as soon as darkness fell.

"No idea at all, except that he's dead," Bare said.

"And he only has one ear," Herk said. "That's in the prophecies too, don't forget."

Harlan's face fell. "I knew a fellow once, who was at least sort of a hero to me, and he's dead. But he had both ears the whole time I knew him."

"Not the right fellow. No, not at all," Herk said. "Couldn't be."

"A one-eared dead hero. Hard to come by," said Harlan. "But I knew a man with a wooden leg called Smith, once . . ."

"What did he call his other leg?" Bare asked eagerly. "That's in the prophecies too, you know."

"It's also an ancient gag," said Sid in disgusted tones.

"As well it should be," replied Herk. "It's an ancient prophecy."

From off in the night, where the watchfires of a hundred circling camps glittered in the darkness, there came the sound of marching feet. The marching stopped, and a few seconds later came a crashing fusillade of gunfire. The marching feet moved on, getting closer.

The marching sound stopped again; there was another moment of quiet and once more the sound of gunshots.

Then the marching started again, and again it

halted, but this time no shots were fired. After a brief silence, the cadenced footsteps began again, and came closer.

"Oh, no," Bare said. "It's started."

"What's started?" Harlan asked.

"The Terror," said Herk. "It's Malfruddin, of course. We taught him the truth, but he pretended not to see it. Now he's shooting everyone we talk to. He's trying to make sure our story doesn't get out."

"Wait a minute," said Harlan. "Who's Malfruddin?"

But Herk and Bare had vanished into the night.

Harlan sat beside his fire, toasting another marshmallow. "This is going to be inconvenient," he remarked to Sid. "I'd hate to get shot now that I've seen the Mall in the distance. A day, maybe two, and we could be there."

Too late. The marching feet were coming. Soon a squad of soldiers wheeled into view, all of them wearing saffron robes and turbans, and clutching Galil Assault Rifles. Their leader was a man brandishing an old-fashioned cavalry saber, and wearing a truly striking earring—not only was it golden and gaudily bejewelled, but a whole other ear hung from it as well.

"Ratner!" Harlan said, jumping to his feet. "What are you doing here? I thought we were going to meet back at the Gypsy encampment."

"Loola and I got tired of waiting," Ratner said. "So we jumped in a Plonkomatic that someone had left sitting there with the keys in it, and drove over to look for you."[1]

"Did you find the Mall?"

"Ah, no," Ratner said. "But that reminds me . . ."

He stepped aside, and turned to the men in his squad. "Present arms!" he shouted. "Ready!"

The squad brought their rifles to their shoulders.

"Aim!"

A dozen rifle barrels pointed directly at Harlan's head.

"Ah, Ratner," Harlan said. "What's this all about?"

"You have to answer a question," Ratner said, rather apologetically. "If you answer it right, then nothing happens to you."

Harlan nodded. "I see. Just for the sake of argument, let's say that I mess up and give the wrong answer."

"Then we shoot you," Ratner explained. "Listen, I didn't make up the silly rules. I'm just carrying them out."

"Who *did* make up the silly rules?"

"When you answer the question, I'll tell you. Okay, now: is there really a Megaverse Mall, or is it all in the mind of some dead hero?"

Just then, Sid the amorphoid fleshopod rose from his seat beside the campfire to put another spare tire on the coals. The firelight illuminated his pseudofeatures with a ruddy glow.

"Keester!" Ratner exclaimed. "What are you doing here?"

---

[1] An astute reader will have noticed that Ratner is lying. He's still under the influence of the Earring of Erk, helped out in this case by the Curse of Amnesiac Finkhood.

"Ah, what did you call me?" Sid asked.

Ratner paled. "Oh, pardon, exalted one! Mister Keester Button, Lord Exalted of the Knights of the True Mall, *Sir*! What are you doing here?" As an aside to Harlan, who was looking very puzzled indeed, Ratner added, "This is Malfruddin's Number Two man. Very important."

While Sid wasn't exactly a rocket scientist, the current situation was easy enough for him to figure out. "Ah, um, why don't you all go home?" he asked Ratner. "And before you go, tell Harlan here the right answer. You know how dogoids are—they always forget the important things."

"Sir, yes Sir!" Ratner shouted, coming to quivering attention and throwing a classy salute at the amorphoid fleshopod. "The correct answer is: There is no Mall but the Megaverse Mall, and only Malfruddin knows where it is! Sir!"

"Oh, very well," Sid said, with a tired wave of one handopod. "Now go away."

"Sir, yes Sir!" Harlan shouted. "Right shoulder, arms! Forward to the rear, march!"

The squad of troops tramped off in the direction from which they had come, singing a sprightly marching song.

"Well, that's over," Sid said, sitting back down by the campfire and pushing a marshmallow onto a stick for himself. "I wonder who they thought I was?"

"I don't know," Harlan said. He frowned out into the darkness beyond the firelight. "Hmmm.

Do you think I should go tell Ratner that he seems to have a werewolf following him?"

"Probably not," Sid opined. "I don't think that he'd have a sense of humor about it."

Chapter 13

The Hero with Only One Ear

Some came walking and some came lame,
  Some came dancing in Loola's name,
But buying and selling was her game . . .
                                    —Blind Grapefruit

Ratner arrived back at the Really Big Dance
Hall just as Don Boethius and the Consolations—
three guys on tenor kazoos and a mixolodian—
struck up the Charleston. The Consolations, like
Stonehenge, were a rock group. They'd started as
a pebble group, but with practice they'd grown
a little boulder. Still, no one listening to them
would take their music for granite.

As the lively music echoed through the hall,
Loola danced up a storm in the middle of the
barnlike building. The storm was a small one,
just big enough to fit inside the Dance Hall,
with hardly enough rain to lay the dust on the
floor (although the lightning sometimes fried a
paying customer). Ratner glanced at the Sun Glo
infrared heaters that had been installed in the
Dance Hall at the insistence of Brother Ojibway
Khartoum, Loola's bald-headed, motorcycle-riding
bodyguard. The heaters made the hall uncomfort-

ably warm for most of the patrons, but if they made Loola happy, Ratner was all for them.

Ever since the gypsy dancer had become the Really Big Dance Hall's major drawing card, "whatever Loola wants, Loola gets," had become the motto of the management. Because when Loola was unhappy, her dancing suffered. Just as an example, attendance at the Dance Hall had sagged for days after Loola dropped out of the Dance Competition on the eve of the regional semifinals.

It wasn't Loola's fault, not really. Gypsy dancers (even reptilian ones) are sensitive and temperamental. Besides, her regular partner, Snake-Spit, wasn't much of a dancer, and the duo probably couldn't have made it past the national quarterfinals anyway.

These days, Loola alternated between dancing with Snake-Spit and mourning her "lost love." Ratner was sure that the phrase had a significant story behind it, but he wasn't quite sure what. He would have thought that Loola's grief was real, if he hadn't once caught her dabbing glycerine under her eyes to make it look like she was crying.

"Well, my hearty," Malfruddin said, as Ratner entered the Dance Hall. "Back early, I see."

"I would have traveled farther," Ratner said, "but I met someone I knew."

"Who was that?"

"Harlan the dogoid," said Ratner.

Malfruddin looked thoughtful. "Wasn't his name Blood, once upon a time?"

"No—Fafner. But his name's not important now."

Before Malfruddin could speak again, Keester Button insinuated himself onto the scene. "Have you extirpated the cult of the hero?" he asked.

Ratner saluted smartly. "As far as I could, Exalted Sublimeness! As you know for yourself, sir!"

"I know for myself?" Keester said in his oiliest tones. "Pray elucidate."

A hope began to beat in Keester's heart.

Perhaps—but no, it couldn't be.

"The wise men said that I would meet my clone at the Mall itself," he muttered under his breath—a habit he'd picked up from Larry Halibut the Self-Referent Werewolf, who had been hanging about the Dance Hall for some time waiting for the full moon, in plain view of everybody except Ratner. "So the Mall is a real place, and not some kind of imaginary figment."

"In any case, Highest of the High," Ratner continued, using Keester's favorite form of address, "when I saw you tonight at the tent of Harlan the dogoid, and you told me to hie myself hence, I did not hesitate, but did my duty. Sir!"

"Ah," was all Keester said, but he was thinking faster than ever before. "The Plonkomatic was here, behind this very Dance Hall," he said to himself. "My clone must be near."[1]

"So other than that," continued Ratner, "I ques-

---

[1]He was right, of course, but for the wrong reason. Being right for the wrong reason is sinful, in a number of obscure ways, but nowhere near as much fun as most sin is, so let's ignore it. Never mind.

tioned every wanderer in the Parking Lot that I could find. Those who believed heretical things, I shot, and those who believed true things, I fined heavily. Thus did I do your will, O Great Keester Button, in order that Malfruddin might be exalted."

"You exacted levies in my name?" Malfruddin asked.

Ratner nodded. "Heavy levies."

"What of the false cults?"

"They are extirpated."

"And the true cults?"

"Enervated."

At that moment, Larry Halibut sprang.

The Gypsy Werewolf and Onetime Hack Novelist had been following Ratner for quite some time, waiting for him to stand still on a night with a full moon, and this was it. As the werewolf made his leap, however, he went past Loola. She made a grab for him, caught him, swung him high and low, and whirled him across the floor to a Liszt waltz that Don Boethius and the Consolations were thumping out in oom-pah style up on the bandstand.

It was a considerably dizzier werewolf who finally tore himself free and got to Ratner, just as Keester and Malfruddin were turning away. With slashing sweeps of his wolfish fangs, Larry Halibut did his work. He dashed out the door with the Earring—and a good bit more—dangling from his jaws.

Keester turned back to Ratner. "Hmmm," he said. "Your ear seems to have gone missing. You'll have to grow your hair long to cover the bare spot."

Out on the dance floor someone screamed. "It's him!"

Then the refrain was taken up by the entire hall. "It's him, it's him! The Hero Without an Ear!"

Chapter 14

The Naked—or at Least the Partially Unclad—Truth

Pain, oh pain, oh endless pain,
It's pain, oh pain, oh endless pain.
Well it's pain, oh pain, it's endless pain,
You see what endless pain can do.
—Blind Grapefruit

Off in the Neitherworld, in the Riverfront Spam-shop, Sdark continued to torture Melvinge.

"You boys have fun, now," Ruth said. She stood, and went over to the door. On the threshold of the Spamshop, she paused to look back at Melvinge. "Cheer up," she said. "It's all in your attitude."

Melvinge, caught in the clutches of hideous, revolting agony, didn't bother to wave good-bye.

"Your friend has deserted you," Sdark said, "and now you will know the wrath of the Card Shark. Nod your head once if you understand."

Even though Melvinge had no desire to nod or do anything else that Sdark wanted, he felt his head go up and down so violently that it bounced off the table.

"Oh, very good," Sdark said. "We are going to have so much fun here, I just know it."

A blind man clutching an old guitar walked in the door of the Spamshop and took a seat on the other side of the room. He counted out a handful of kropotniks from the pocket of his patched and faded jeans, then ordered. The waiter brought him a plate of deep-fried Spam and a glass of water. After the man had eaten, he began to pick a slow, bluesy tune on his guitar, and sing a mournful ballad. Melvinge was too preoccupied to pay much attention.

Perhaps the only thing more painful than torture is reading about it, so while Sdark is having his fun with Melvinge, let us once again turn to the Parking Lot of the Megaverse Mall.

The chilly rain had ended sometime after midnight, so Harlan and Sid packed up the tent, stowed Melvinge's body, and hit the road again. A supercharged yellow Dusenberg pulled up alongside them, its headlights gleaming.

"Is this the way to the Mall?" the driver asked.

"Yeah, just keep going," Harlan answered. "You'll get there."

"Thanks, pal," said the driver, and pulled away again.

"What else could I say?" Harlan muttered as the Dusenberg's crimson taillights faded into the darkness.

Just then a fellow ran up, heading in the opposite direction. "He's come!" the man shouted. "He's here! The Hero with Only One Ear has arrived! He will lead us to the Mall!"

"Where? Where?" Harlan shouted.

But the man had already run off to spread the good news. A little farther along, a cluster of people holding Tiki Torches had gathered around the tailfins of a '63 Chevy. "He has come," one of the people said as Harlan and Sid walked up, with Melvinge still strapped onto the fleshopod's back.

"Don't listen to them!" a man said in a disgusted tone. "This One-Eared Hero is a crock. There's only one way to get to the Mall, and that's by being chosen the All-Parking-Lot Long-Distance Spitting Champion!"

"Long-distance spitting?" Harlan asked. "I thought it was supposed to be a dance contest that would get you to the Mall."

"Lies and false doctrine," the man said. "That's a heretical story spread by Sdark to lure the faithful from the chance to find Really Big Bargains and make Wise Purchasing Decisions at the Megaverse Mall. Sure, it sounds good, a Dance Contest, and it's got enough truth in it that people will believe it. There really is a Contest! But not Dance, no sir!"

"And the real contest is . . ." Harlan began.

"Long-Distance Spitting! Watch!" The man projected a stream of tobacco juice from the enormous chaw in his cheek. The wad was still rising in a perfect ballistic arc when it was lost to view, out of the light of the torches.

"That's very impressive," commented Sid.

"There you go," said the man. "Proves that there's only one way to get to the Megaverse Mall, and that's by spitting for it. If you spit far enough, one of the Mall Security Personnel will come for you and escort you to the Main Entrance where the Mall Directory is located."

"Come off it, old man," said a woman near the

edge of the crowd. "If spitting was all it took, you'd have been in the Mall years ago. There's something more than spitting: you also gotta have good directions. Spitting *and* good directions, that's the ticket." And with that, she too spat out a wad that flew far beyond the circle of light.

"Good directions are enough," said another. "Look—these cars all once contained people who aren't here anymore. Where are they? They must still be in the Mall, shopping. Otherwise they would have gotten into their cars and left."

A rumbling sound came from beneath the asphalt of the parking lot. The sound grew nearer, and louder. A huge dorsal fin popped through the blacktop, cut along for a few yards, then vanished again as its owner submerged.

"Loan Shark," someone whispered. "Perhaps Sdark himself."

"The Loan Sharks put up the money to build the Mall," said the spitting champion. "But they don't want anyone to reach it. That way, the Mall will default on its loans, and the Loan Sharks will own it all."

"Loan Sharks can't create," said another voice, one that Harlan found familiar. "They only put up money so that others can create. But beware, once they have you in their power!"

The speaker stepped into the circle of lantern light. It was Herk, with Bare right beside him. "Loan Sharks are real," Herk said. "And if Loan Sharks are real, then the Mall also must be real!"

"You tell it!" exclaimed Sid. The amorphoid fleshopod came forward and addressed the crowd.

"People!" he said. "What he told you is true! I was in the clutches of Sdark the Loan Shark, and he had me in his power. He had me stuck by the side of the highway. But I defeated him, and now I'm on my way to the Megaverse Mall!"

"Only those who wear the garments of perfection can enter the Megaverse Mall," said Bare. "And those who wear the clothes from other Malls betray their lack of faith. For in the Megaverse Mall there are both Thrift Stores and Fashionable Boutiques, where we shall be able to buy glorious raiment!"

"Amen!" shouted a voice from the back, and a shirt came sailing out of the dark as its owner ripped it off. "When I come to the Megaverse Mall, I'll have no need of things bought anywhere else!"

"The Mall is within us all," added Herk, but he spoke quietly. "Wherever we are, as long as we're spending money, the Mall is there too. It doesn't matter if we're clothed or not—but don't tell that to my friend."

"Say *what*?" chorused a group of very confused passersby.

"Dancing! Dancing will take us there!" shouted another woman. She picked up castanets and began to sashay up the street, forming the head of an enormous conga line as others dropped what they were doing to follow her.

"Ptooi," said the champion spitter. "You won't get to the Mall by dancing even if you hoof it for the rest of your life."

Chapter 15

Comings and Goings in the Really Big Dance Hall

Heard a mighty rumbling way under the ground,
Must have been Sdark, a-cruising around.
"Momma, momma, oh what comes now?"
"Gonna get to the Mall, but I don't know how."
—Blind Grapefruit

Back in the Really Big Dance Hall, shouts of "The Hero with Only One Ear!" echoed from the cracked and rusty walls.

"You traitor!" Malfruddin snarled, pointing at Ratner. "Are you trying to throw me out and take over?"

"No, no!" Ratner cried. "It isn't my fault, I didn't do it, this isn't what I meant at all!"

"The Hero with Just One Ear," Keester muttered behind his hand. "There must be a way to make a buck out of this one."

While they spoke, and while cries of "The Hero! The Hero!" still resounded through the hall, Larry the Unemployed Werewolf had gone streaking out the door. In all the confusion and hysteria, nobody noticed a grey and blurry wolf-shape with Ratner's ear clutched fast between its teeth.

Outside the Really Big Dance Hall, Larry

paused to look around. He knew that he would have to get the Earring of Erk back to Novaleen the Gypsy Queen, but how?

Stepping into a convenient phone booth, he changed back to a mild-mannered novelist. Then he went out into the darkened Parking Lot. Removing the Earring from its pair of well-attached ears seemed to be the essential problem right now, and Larry had an idea about how to do it.

"A nice pot of ear goulash," he said, stepping cheerfully along. "Let it simmer for a few days, and that ring is going to drop right off."

He walked into the dark Parking Lot in search of a kettle to borrow. But before he had gone very far in the direction of the nearest tent city, where a band of itinerant perfumers were colognizing the Parking Lot, he was surrounded by a pack of people who all rushed up to him chanting "He is Bare! He is Bare!"

Larry looked down. Sure enough, in the excitement, he'd forgotten to recover his clothing. But somehow that didn't seem quite enough to explain the reaction he was getting. Then he noticed that the people who surrounded him were unclothed too.

"Lead us, Master!" one of the crowd shouted. "Lead us to the Mall!"

"Wait a cotton-picking minute!" Larry yelled, all thoughts of borrowing a goulash pan vanishing. "What are you talking about?"

"You're wearing your Bare-shirt," a man said, prostrating himself before the astonished werewolf. "You know the way to the Mall! Lead us, and we will follow!"

Larry eyed the large and growing group around him. They were pressing forward, hands reaching out.

"Ah, look over there!" Larry cried, his hand shooting out and pointing back over their heads. When those in front turned to follow his pointing finger, Larry, too, turned—and wisely fled in the other direction.

Some of the more observant members of the mob noticed that he was fading into the distance.

"There he goes!" someone shouted. "Follow him!"

The mob began to stream after the departing werewolf, still shouting, "To the Mall! To the Mall!" With the zealots in hot pursuit, Larry ran back into the Really Big Dance Hall, where another crowd had surrounded Ratner and begun chanting "One-Ear! One-Ear!"

The werewolf dived for cover. Rolling under the bandstand where Boethius and the Consolations were striking up a quickstep, he changed back into a wolf and crouched there, holding the ears in his teeth. Out on the dance floor, he could hear what sounded like a riot in progress. Shouts of "Bare!" and "Ear!" mingled with the crash of breaking furniture.

Out front, Ojibway Khartoum and the Motorcycle Monks formed up into a flying wedge and went wading into the fray, trying to reach Loola. The Gypsy Princess, oblivious to the mayhem around her, was still dancing with Snake-Spit in the center of the hall. The saffron-jacketed monks snatched her from her partner's arms and bore her out of the crowd to safety.

Down beneath the bandstand, Larry the Werewolf felt something snap around his neck. It was a collar, attached to a leash. The leash was held by a lady with a henna-red beehive hairdo. What little light there was in Larry's refuge glittered off of her rhinestone sunglasses.

"Rowf?" Larry said, his wolfish throat unable to come closer to words.

"No," said the lady. "Ruth. Let's go for a walk, Larry. You have something I need."

Chapter 16

Ratner on the Run

Oh, One-Eared Man, where you gonna run to?
Oh, One-Eared Man, where you gonna run to?
Oh, One-Eared Man, where you gonna run to, all
  on that day?"

—Blind Grapefruit

Meanwhile, out on the dance floor, Ratner decided that this was a good time to be moving along. Now that he'd fallen out of favor with Malfruddin, waiting around here wasn't going to bring him any closer to the largest Food Court in the Megaverse.

Taking advantage of the shouts and confusion, he insinuated himself through a newly opened crack in the wall of the dance hall, nearly tripping over a blind street singer on his way out. He snatched the man's floppy hat as he passed and pulled it down over his missing ear.

Beyond the walls of the Dance Hall, rows of parked cars spread out in every direction in the light of the false dawn. Secure in his disguise, Ratner casually stepped on into the Parking Lot. A crowd of onlookers had gathered outside the Really Big Dance Hall.

"The Megaverse Mall has been found," he heard one man say, "and a Loan Shark owns it."

"Then all things belong to the Loan Sharks," another said, "and there is no hope."

"No," said another. "A One-Eared Man will appear, and he will lead us to the One True Mall."

"That's what you said last week about the Dance Contest," his companion replied, "and look where it got you."

"It got me a third-place ribbon," said the first speaker. "That's better than anyone else has gotten. In the Megaverse Mall, all the ribbons will be First Prize, and the contests will go on night and day!"

"I don't think the Mall even exists," said his companion. "It's just a story made up to get people to places like the Really Big Dance Hall."

"Then what the heck are you still doing here?" demanded the other. "Why don't you just go back to your car and drive away?"

"That's where I'm heading. Have you seen a '32 Hupmobile with a bunch of plastic flowers on the antenna? I know I left it somewhere around here."

Ratner walked on. *All good stuff to remember,* he thought. *When Malfruddin comes into his own, he'll want to know who's been saying things like that. And maybe he'll reward me for finding out, and bring me with him to the Mall.*

At last, Ratner came to a tent pitched between two cars. A dogoid and an amorphoid fleshopod lay there, asleep in the lee of a pile of tarpaulin-covered boxes and cartons serving as a wind-break.

"Keester!" Ratner whispered to himself. "Back here already!" Then, "No. I left Keester in the Dance Hall. So it must be *another* amorphoid fleshopod—but who?"

The answer came to him in a flash of what Herk or Bare would have instantly recognized as revelation.

"Of course! This must be Sid!"

And a memory stirred in his gypsy-curse-blasted mind, only to be sandbagged before it could be fully developed, for the curses of Novaleen the Gypsy Queen had range and striking power and time on target.

"Harlan," Ratner said, poking the dog. "Harlan, wake up. I have to talk to you."

Harlan stirred and sat up. "Wow," he said. "Have I been having some weird dreams!"

"Harlan," said Ratner. "We've been buddies for a long time. Tell me, what do you know about Herk and Bare?"

"They showed up and walked through here last night," Harlan fibbed. "Never saw them before, never saw them again. Why?"

"They were the ones who started all this stuff about the One-Eared Man. I have to ask them some questions. All of a sudden it's gotten very important to me."

"All I know is they went off that-a-way," Harlan said. He gestured west, away from the Dance Hall. "What's up?"

Ratner looked about nervously. "Promise not to tell anybody?"

"Yeah sure," Harlan said. He leaned back against Melvinge's body, which was once again serving as a centerpole for the improvised tent. "Shoot."

"I think *I* might be the One-Eared Man." And Ratner pulled off his hat, and showed that it was so.

"Whoo-wee!" Harlan said. "That's a nasty one. What happened?"

"I was wearing an earring over there."

"Don't tell me; a werewolf snatched it."

"How did you know that?" Ratner demanded.

Harlan shrugged. "Just a lucky guess. You know, there's a real chance that you could turn into a werewolf too."

"Stop trying to cheer me up," Ratner said morosely.

"Melvinge was a werewolf, you know," continued Harlan. "He's dead now, of course. A silver bullet got him. Got to watch out for those silver bullets."

"Maybe a holy man could lift the curse off me," suggested Ratner—whose mind, understandably, remained fixed on his own problems. "Someone like Herk or Bare, maybe."

"Those are the holiest guys I've ever seen," Harlan agreed.

"The only hole those guys have is in their heads," Sid put in.

"Shut up," Harlan and Ratner advised in stereo.

"I have to find them," Ratner continued alone.

"You know," Sid commented, "after the way you

were looking to kill them just last night, they might be kind of hard for you to locate."

Ratner looked disappointed. "I hadn't thought of that."

"I guess not," Sid agreed.

"Meanwhile, I'm still looking for the One True Mall," Harlan said. "I think it's to the east, so that's where I'm heading."

"Well, good luck to you," said Ratner. "But I've got to find Herk and Bare." He stood up and faded away to the west.

When he was entirely out of sight, Sid pulled up the bottom of the tarp and knocked on one of the boxes it concealed.

"It's okay to come out now," he said. "He's gone."

"Thank goodness," said Herk, rising to his full height and stretching. "It was tight in there."

"Indubitably," said Bare, pushing the lid of the box entirely aside as he also stood.

"You don't suppose that Ratner *is* the true One-Eared Man?" Herk asked Bare as he helped his companion climb out of the box.

"No," Bare replied. "For the One-Eared Man is good, and Ratner is, at best, so-so."

"Besides," said Harlan as he took down the top of the tent, "didn't you say that the One-Eared Man was dead?"

He tucked the tarp into his pack and started to hoist Melvinge's corpse onto Sid's back. "Give me a hand with the boss, and let's get out of here."

Chapter 17

New Developments in the Neitherworld

Sdark's found new and wondrous things to do.
I said, Sdark's found new and wondrous things to do.
If you don't watch out, he might do them to you.
> —Blind Grapefruit

Meanwhile, in the Neitherworld, Sdark had been tormenting Melvinge at a corner booth of the Riverfront Spamshop for an eternity or so.[1] Even exquisite agony can lose its novelty if it goes on long enough—Melvinge was hurting badly, but not so badly that he hadn't long since become bored by it all.

He caught himself stifling a yawn. At the same moment, Sdark stifled a yawn of his own.

"I'll make you hurt for the rest of time," the Card Shark growled, embarrassed to be caught in a moment of inattention.

"If that's the best you can do," said Melvinge, yawning again, "I don't even want to hear about it."

"All right, then—try *this*!" Sdark exclaimed, and shot Melvinge with the brace of M-79s, blowing him clear through the back wall of the Spamshop.

And once again, Melvinge died.

---

[1] Give or take a couple of months.

Chapter 18

Just a Ping-Pong Ball in the Game Room of the Megaverse

Oh young Melvinge, oh young Melvinge,
The One-Eared Man,
Oh, young Melvinge, the One-Eared Man,
Just you watch out for Ratner, 'cause he has a plan.
—Blind Grapefruit

One moment Melvinge felt himself being turned into dogmeat in the Neitherworld by Sdark's grenade launchers, and the next moment he woke up standing in a vast concrete field covered with parked cars. Guy ropes led out from him in different directions. He looked skyward, and saw that he was holding up the center of a plastic tarp.

"What the heck?" Melvinge muttered.

He reached up to feel for his ear, and was relieved to find that it was still missing. "I guess that means I'm still me."

He glanced around. Parked cars and other vehicles stretched from horizon to horizon.

"The Parking Lot!" he exclaimed. "Maybe I can find the Megaverse Mall after all."

He untangled himself from the tent, and walked out into the traffic lane between the rows of parked cars.

A tyrannasauroid hot-dog vendor spotted him. "Hey, sport!" the creature yelled, waving a char-broiled dachshund on a poppyseed bun. "Get yer red-hots here!"

Then the large reptile looked at him more closely. "Oh, wow!" it exclaimed. "The One-Eared Man!"

"Honest," Melvinge began, "I'm not Vincent Van Gogh!"

But before Melvinge could finish explaining, a half ton of creamed cauliflower fell out of the sky and smashed him to the pavement.

The killer stepped forward, the release line to the skyhook from which the cauliflower had been suspended still held loosely in one hand. "Nobody tries to horn in on my racket," the assassin said. "I'm the only One-Eared Man there is, or my name isn't Ratner!"

Abruptly, Melvinge found himself back in the Neitherworld, sitting in the rubble of a wall out-side the Riverfront Spamshop. He shook his head to clear away the lingering traces of cream sauce. "I knew my good luck couldn't last," he muttered.

He considered looking inside the Spamshop to see if Sdark was still there, but decided against it. Instead, he lit out for the bus stop. "Time to get out of town," he told himself. "If there *is* an 'out of town' here in the Neitherworld."

Fairly soon a bus came along: the Clement of Alexandria—Origen Route, it said. The adver-tising signs on its side urged him to Buy Orca Cola for That Chew Me Up Taste.

The bus came to a stop with a screech of brakes.

The door sighed open. Melvinge mounted the steps and slid into a seat. The driver pulled away from the curb, and the Riverfront Spamshop disappeared into the distance. Soon the bus was rolling along a tree-lined lane into the open countryside.

Melvinge looked at the driver. The fellow seemed oddly familiar. Those broad shoulders, that pallid grey skin, those gill slits in his neck . . .

"Surprise, sucker," Sdark said. "Have a nice trip."

He stood and wriggled out of one of the side windows, leaving the driver's seat empty.

"I wonder how he did that," said Melvinge. The side window was too small for Melvinge to get through, let alone someone as large as the Card Shark.

Then Melvinge had other things to wonder about, like where the bus was going and how he was going to get off. Up ahead, through the front windows, he could see the trees ending. Beyond them, and rapidly approaching, a straight line against the sky marked the edge of what had to be a cliff.

"Oh, fudge," Melvinge said, unknowingly echoing Harlan's favorite expletive. He dashed forward and tried to turn the steering wheel. It came off in his hands.

The bus hurtled off the edge of the cliff. Had someone been watching, all he would have heard before a tremendous smash sounded from the bottom would have been a fading, wailing cry of "Oh, *fuuuuuuuuuudge!*"

Melvinge woke, sat up, opened his eyes, and turned his head. The hot tarmac, the Grape Nehi Soda cans, the blowing dust, the rancid cauliflower—all of that could only mean that he was back in the Parking Lot. He stood up, slowly.

A few yards away, the tyrannosauroid hot-dog vendor saw Melvinge get up, and yelled, "He is the one! He is the one! I have seen him rise from the dead!"

The Tyrannosauroid galloped off, knocking over a cage of German Shepherds on the way.

"Ein feste Burg ist unser Gott," sang the Shepherds, while their sheep joined in the chorus with "Bah, bah, bah."

"Come and see! Come and bear witness!" shouted the Tyrannosauroid, waving its barbecue fork as it ran.

"Loony-tune," Melvinge said, as the Tyrannosauroid disappeared behind a line of parked cars. "I don't need trouble like this."

He turned and began to run in the opposite direction.

Not much time had passed before he was aware of pounding footsteps on the tarmac behind him. He glanced back over his shoulder. A man was following him, someone who looked vaguely familiar. Melvinge slowed down and then stopped, wishing that the time he'd spent in the Neitherworld hadn't dulled his memory so much.

He knew that this man was important—although the last time Melvinge remembered seeing him (which had been on a playing card back during that blackjack game with Sdark), the guy had still had both ears. Now he only had one.

Melvinge shrugged. *There's a lot of that going around, I guess.*

"Hi, Ratner," Melvinge said.

"Do I know you from somewhere?" Ratner said, his memories of Melvinge destroyed by the Gypsy Curse. "Not that it's important. Could you hold this for a minute?"

He handed Melvinge a custard cream pie.

"Ah, sure," Melvinge began. "What's . . ."

"Don't have time to talk, gotta run," Ratner said, dashing off.

Melvinge turned, and saw a female grizzly bear approaching, a cub tagging along behind her. *Uh oh,* Melvinge thought. *Better not get between her and her cub.*

Then Melvinge noticed that someone had apparently hit the cub in the face with a custard pie, a pie just like the one he was holding. *Uh oh,* Melvinge thought again, and then the bear was upon him.

Suddenly Melvinge found himself looking out through a jumble of broken glass and twisted steel. He was sitting in a ruined bus at the bottom of a cliff. He crawled slowly out of the wreckage, being careful not to cut himself on the sharp edges, and saw that he was on a dusty plain. The cliff rising behind him stretched to the horizon in either direction. He was back in the Neitherworld.

Now what do I do? he wondered. *Walk straight ahead, or try to climb the cliff?*

Melvinge shook his head. *Climb a cliff, just to*

get back to Trenton? He started walking forward.

The plain was flat, and covered with waving grass mingled with little white flowers. Here and there a stand of trees rose up to break the monotony. A gentle breeze ruffled Melvinge's hair where it protruded from under his beanie.

Melvinge ambled along, feeling good about himself. Maybe strolling through this gardenlike place would eventually prove as boring as the rest of the Neitherworld, but at least for the present it was restful.

So it happened that Melvinge wasn't watching his step, and fell into a pit which had been covered with branches and leaves. More surprised than hurt, he looked up from the bottom of the pit. The sides were high, but they didn't look impossible to climb—and then the light from the sky was blocked out by the looming, broad-shouldered shape of Sdark.

"Hello, Mel," Sdark said.

The Card Shark held out an anvil in his big, finlike hands and dropped it onto Melvinge's upturned face.

Without thinking Melvinge rolled away, only to find that he was rolling on oily pavement and not cool dirt.

What do you know, he thought. *Sdark must have gotten me again.*

Melvinge looked around. His roll away from the anvil (which must not have worked soon enough, he realized, or else he wouldn't be back here in the Parking Lot again) had taken him under some kind of car. The bottom of the car had a little label

122

punched directly into the metal: Made with Pride by Union Elves.

Melvinge could hear people talking beside the car.

"Where did he go?" asked one voice. "He was here just a minute ago."

"It must be true," said a second voice. "The One-Eared Man has come back to life!"

"What did he look like?" asked a third voice.

"A skinny blond guy," said the first voice. "With a striped shirt and a beanie."

I have to get rid of these clothes, Melvinge thought as he squirmed out from under the car on the side away from the muttering crowd.

Ducking low to keep out of sight, he sconkered off through two rows of parked vehicles. Up ahead, lying in a pile between a Reo and an Oldsmobile, he spotted a whole pile of discarded clothing. *Today must be my lucky day,* he thought, going over and pawing through the jetsam for some duds that looked like they might fit.

He found a T-shirt with the legend *My Parents Went to The Really Big Dance Hall™ and All They Bought Me Was a Lousy Shirt*, and a pair of Don't Tell My Secret^R jeans with padded hips.

Melvinge stripped out of his old clothes. He was about to get dressed again when a strange sound pierced the air. High and shrill the notes echoed among the deserted cars.

"A calliope!" he exclaimed in delighted recognition. "A steam calliope!"

Melvinge tried to remember the name of tune it was playing. " 'The Natural Album March'?" he muttered. " 'The Tarzan's Tripes Forever'?" Then suddenly it hit him. " 'Here Come the Clones!' " he shrieked in childish glee.

A crunching sound came to him over the evening air—a slow, metallic crunch that brought back painful memories of the bottom of a cliff. He looked up. The Steam Calliope was being played at the top of a Steam Roller, a monstrous metal roller crunching down the row of cars toward him. It was almost on top of him, and he hadn't even got his pants on.

"Oh, no," Melvinge sighed. He closed his eyes.

He wasn't at all surprised, when he opened them again, to see that he was at the bottom of a pit, standing on top of an anvil. With the anvil under him, the edge of the pit was only a foot or so above his head.

He jumped, and pulled himself back up onto the plain. Ahead of him, under a weeping willow tree, stood a table. Two people, a man and a woman, sat there playing cards. The man looked up as Melvinge approached.

"Here, boy—there's a lady present. Dress yourself!"

Melvinge blushed. "I'm afraid I don't *have* any clothes."

"Look in my carpetbag," the man replied. "I think I have a spare set."

Melvinge did as he was told. Soon he was dressing himself in a natty set of pinstripes, not unlike those that had been worn by Sdark. The resemblance made him a bit uneasy, but he told himself it wasn't nice to criticize a generous action.

When he was properly clothed again, he approached the table. "Hello," he said. "My name is Melvinge."

"Indeed?" said the man. "I would have guessed that you were Vincent Van Gogh. But never mind that. My name is Crater, Judge Crater. The lady is Amelia Earhart."

"Pleased to make your acquaintance," Amelia said. "My goodness, with three people again, maybe we can play something besides War."

"Things have been rather dull since little Kaspar Hauser left," Judge Crater confided, "but we'll have lots of fun now. How do you feel about a nice game of Go Fish?"

Chapter 19

Some Important Things Are Restored, and Others Revealed

The Megaverse maidens tell stories and sing
  The songs about Melvinge, their Parking-Lot King,
Way out on the Interstate, long long ago,
  When a man's only hope was a mean dosey-doe . . .
                    —Blind Grapefruit

Larry Halibut, the Hack Novelist and Part-time Werewolf, wasn't happy. He had a collar on his neck, a leash attached to the collar, and the henna-haired lady called Ruth at the other end of the leash. In spite of his efforts to resist, she led him away from the Really Big Dance Hall, where the followers of Bare and One-Ear still swirled about in furious disputation, and out into the night.

"You won't be able to turn back into a person until I take that collar off, you know," Ruth said. "It *is* a wolf collar."

"Ruff," complained Larry, who had a deadline to meet on Number Fifteen in the *Stupid World* series, and knew he couldn't type fast enough with his paws.

"I know it's rough," said the three-hundred-year-old Perfect Master, "but that's the way it has to be." She looked at the pair of ears, linked by the Earring, that she held in her hand. "Now to get this ear-bob back to its rightful owner before it's too late."

Without warning, a thrown rock cracked the windshield of a car beside Ruth and Larry. "Schismatic!" cried a voice out of a nearby mob of Mall-seekers. "Halvah eater!"

"Oh, dear," said Ruth. "We'd better hurry. These sectarian disputes can get quite nasty."

"Brothers, we must be wary," called out another voice from within the mob. "Sdark is always among us, trying to keep us from finding the One True Mall."

"Don't listen to him!" yelled the first voice. "He's wearing a fake Bare-shirt!"

The mob parted for a second, long enough for Larry to glimpse the two rival zealots: a small man wearing a T-shirt emblazoned with the word Bare, and a second man who wore no shirt at all. Larry eyed their ears speculatively—the man in the cloth Bare-shirt had a particularly outstanding pair. It had been quite a while since the werewolf had been able to whip up a cauldron of ear goulash, and it looked like Ruth wasn't going to give him either of the ears she currently possessed.

Meanwhile, the dispute between the two groups of Mall-seekers had degenerated into shouts of "Am not!"—"Are, too!"—"Am *not!*" Ruth turned her attention back to the Earring.

"Let's see if I remember how this works," she said as she fiddled with the clasp. "You turn the little knob one way if the true wearer is alive, and the other way if he's dead. Now let's see. Can't take it off that way ... hmmm ... can't take it off *that* way, either. He's alive? Wait a minute. There it comes. He's dead again."

"Rrow?" said Larry, baffled. Dead then alive then dead? Oh, well. It didn't matter. What mattered was that Ruth now had an ear loose in her hand. Much as Larry hated to degrade himself that way, he went into a wolfish sit-up-and-beg routine, whimpering and staring at the ear.

"No, Larry, that one's not for you," Ruth said. "I have to give it back to its rightful owner. He needs it."

At that very moment, the Earring's rightful owner was sitting under a willow tree in the Neitherworld, playing a game of Go Fish with Judge Crater and Amelia Earhart.

Earhart, Melvinge wondered. *Could that be significant? Ear-hart. Ear. And how about the game? Go Fish. Fish?*

Melvinge looked over at the judge. Something didn't seem right about him. What was it? The uncanny luck that he had with his cards? His mouth full of sharp-edged triangular teeth?

Amelia Earhart looked at Melvinge over the upper rim of her sunglasses, the ones with the rhinestones.

"Your play," she said.

All at once, Melvinge understood. He threw down his cards and pointed at Judge Crater.

"I know you," he said. "You're Sdark!"

The judge stood up, overturning the table and spilling the cards onto the grass. His tailored suit ripped open as he began to expand. His eyes turned to flat black shark eyes, his skin to rough sharkskin.

"You found me," he said, "but it won't do you any good. You're mine!"

The Card Shark leaned forward as if to seize the hapless Melvinge and slice through him with those razorblade rows of glistening teeth. At that moment, Amelia—whose hair, Melvinge suddenly noticed, was a bright henna-red—handed Melvinge an earring.

"Quick," she said. "Put this on."

Melvinge reached for his ear (remembering at the last moment to reach for his left ear, since his right one was still missing). The Earring went on, and once again it began to work its fabled magic. He became devious and clever,[1] and the nature of reality shifted around him. Instead of being dead in the Neitherworld, he was alive and being carried on the back of an amorphoid fleshopod—his old acquaintance Sid—heading through the night at a jogging trot toward a huge structure in the middle distance.

"Let me down!" shouted Melvinge. "I can walk!"

"Huh?" Sid said. "You're supposed to be dead."

"Oh, please," Melvinge said, the deviousness of the Earring already hard at work. "Dead people don't get seasick—which is what I'm about to be all over your head if you don't stop moving and let me off."

---

[1] Or at any rate, more devious and clever than he had previously been—which, given that he'd started this adventure with a deviousness level close to zero, was not necessarily a huge amount.

Sid came to a halt, and Melvinge dismounted. As soon as his feet touched the tarmac, he was almost bowled over by Harlan, who leapt upon him in an excess of doggish emotion.

"Oh, wow, Boss, you're alive!" Harlan cried. The dogoid was trying to lick Melvinge's face and talk all at once—a rather slobbery affair.

"Hey, cut it out," Melvinge said. "Look, is Ratner around?"

"Around?" Sid asked. "You betcha. In fact, it's been hard to get rid of him. Why do you want to know?"

"I think he's been trying to kill me," said Melvinge.

"In that case," said Harlan, "you're in trouble—because here he comes now."

"Quick!" said Melvinge cleverly. "Run!"

Sid, Harlan, and Melvinge dashed off through the dark in the direction of the huge, barnlike structure, with Ratner following close behind. Soon another group of people began to run behind them as well, shouting "One-Ear! One-Ear!" as they ran—though it was hard to tell if by this they meant Melvinge or Ratner (since the description could fit either one of them equally well).

"Is that big building up ahead the Mall?" Melvinge asked, puffing along.

"I sure hope so," Harlan replied. "Or else I've schlepped you all over the Parking Lot for nothing."

But as they got closer, Melvinge could see that the sign over the building's front door read Really Big Dance Hall. Melvinge wasn't planning to go in at all—but before he and his companions could jog on by with Ratner and the crowd of zealots in hot pursuit, a hand reached out of the doorway and grabbed Melvinge by the arm.

"You want to dance with the lady? Only a dime a dance."

Melvinge looked at the huge clasp knife Snake-Spit (for it was he) was holding to his navel, and didn't need the Earring of Erk to come up with the right answer to the thug's question.

"Sure do," said Melvinge hastily. "Nothing I want to do more than have a dance. Maybe even two."

"Pay in advance," Snake-Spit said.

He turned Melvinge upside down and shook him, in order to collect all his loose change. Nothing rolled out, since Harlan had long since gone through all of Melvinge's pockets in search of *dinero* to pay for cheese blintzes and mango sodas on the road. Snake-Spit unlimbered the clasp knife again and got ready to show his displeasure in the only way he knew how.

"Hold it," said a familiar voice in Melvinge's remaining ear. It was Ruth, with a werewolf following her at the end of a red leather leash. "I'm paying for this one," she said, and handed the thug a dime.

The three-hundred-year-old Perfect Master turned to Melvinge, reached up, and set something against the right side of his head. He felt a brief tingle as it attached itself (or rather, reattached itself—for it was, in fact, his missing ear). The seekers for the One-Eared Hero turned their attention away from Melvinge, and back entirely to Ratner. The former short-order cook and would-be prophet was promptly mobbed, and soon became entirely lost to sight in the frenzy.

Loola the Gypsy Princess held out her hand. She took Melvinge away into the center of the Dance Hall, and began to dance with him for all she was worth, or for a dime anyway.

The dance soon blossomed into the kind of warm regard that can only come between two lovers long separated.

"Don't I know you from somewhere?" Melvinge asked as they twirled around to the music of Don Boethius.

"I don't know," Loola replied. "You kind of remind me of someone, but he wore a rugby shirt and a beanie. You're wearing a pinstripe suit. Besides, he's dead."

"Guess I'm not him, then," Melvinge said with a shrug.

They danced on, gazing into one another's eyes.

Suddenly, without warning, a tremendous crashing sound came from beneath the Dance Hall. The floor tilted upward, spilling the dancers aside. Out of the depths rose a huge grey creature, with bloodshot red eyes and gnashing jaws filled with multiple rows of teeth. The gill slits on its sides opened and closed with its ponderous breathing.

"Malfruddin!" the creature called, its thunderous tones filling the Really Big Dance Hall. "Malfruddin, you're late with a payment!"

133

Chapter 20

All Kinds of Reunions at the Really Big Dance Hall

Sometimes Sdark wears sharkskin,
  Sometimes Sdark wears a gown.
Sometimes Sdark wears a four-piece suit,
  And walks through the middle of town.
                              —Blind Grapefruit

The Loan Shark raised up horrible and red-eyed in the midst of the wreckage of the Really Big Dance Hall.

Loola and Melvinge clung to each other as concrete floor slabs tilted every which way around them. The bandstand collapsed underneath Don Boethius and the Consolations, giving their listeners a new view of rockin' roll. Everybody in the hall scrambled to get as far away as they could from Malfruddin and Malfruddin's Number Two Man (or fleshopod) Keester Button.

But Malfruddin, in spite of having geeky eyebrows, was not so easily cowed. "What are you talking about?" he demanded of the Loan Shark.

"You borrowed funds to renovate this place," the creature rumbled. "Twenty percent compounded hourly builds up fast."

Then the Loan Shark's eyes fell on Keester Button, where the fleshopod stood beside Malfruddin. The huge creature gave a ponderous, satisfied chuckle, like boulders rolling downhill. "And my old friend Sid!" the Loan Shark said. "You owe me too, Sid."

"I'm not Sid!" protested Keester. "I'm Keester Button!"

"Sure you are. And I'm not really Sdark, either. This is just going to be a bust-up between total strangers. Now pay up, or else!"

"Or else what?" inquired Malfruddin.[1]

"Or else I'm repossessing this Dance Hall and everything in it," said the Loan Shark. To make the point clear, it stretched its enormous jaws open even wider, so that everybody in the hall got a good view of the route leading down into its vast and echoing belly.

Melvinge found the view uncomfortably familiar. In the days before he'd been shot by a silver bullet and sent down to the Neitherworld, he'd spent more time than he liked to remember stranded inside Sdark's vitals. It wasn't an experience he especially cared to repeat, or even one that he wanted to wish on anyone else, except perhaps Ratner (at least for as long as Ratner kept on trying to do him, Melvinge, in).

"Somebody *do* something!" he exclaimed, but

---

[1] An observant member of the crowd might have noticed that Malfruddin didn't appear as frightened by the sudden appearance of the Loan Shark as a sapient being in his position ought to have been. But it's hard to be observant when a Loan Shark is looming over you, and you're staring into a cavernous maw that looks (and smells) like the Holland Tunnel with teeth.

nobody in the Dance Hall came forward to volunteer.

" 'Pay me, oh pay me, pay me my money down,' " the Loan Shark hummed. Its singing voice was rather like the music of a baritone cement mixer. " 'Pay me or go to jail . . . ' "

Then Melvinge had an Inspiration. This was, of course, the influence of the Earring of Erk, now attached to his left earlobe and bestowing upon him all sorts of devious cleverness and knowledge of legal theory. He stepped away from the terrified embrace of Loola, and confronted the fearsome Loan Shark where it loomed over Malfruddin and Keester Button.

"Malfruddin owes you nothing, fish," Melvinge said, "for you have lost all rights to every debt owed you."

"All things were built with the funds of the Loan Sharks," Sdark roared, "and therefore all things rightly belong to us!"

"You are a robber, Sdark," retorted Melvinge (with a bit of help from the Earring), "and have no just cause to demand payment at all. Keester Button owes you nothing. The debt on Pinkie's is owed by Sid—but you have demanded repayment of Keester, who was never in your debt. In doing so, you have transgressed justice. You have been duped, gulled, cheated, and made a fool of, Sdark, and Keester was the cheese in the mousetrap of your undoing. Now go, for your power is broken!"

It was a real pity that Sdark lacked a moustache, for if he'd had one, he would have twirled it. "Curses!" the Loan Shark hissed. "Foiled again! But I'll be back. I'll swallow you and all your works, and digest you too. Your search for the Megaverse Mall is hopeless, for it will belong to *me!*"

With that, the Loan Shark gave a flurry with its tail and vanished beneath the floor.

"Dance, dance!" Malfruddin shouted at the handful of people who remained. "The Hall is mine, the Parking Lot is mine, and soon the Mall shall be mine as well! Dance!"

Amid the wreckage of the bandstand, Don Boethius and the Consolations struck up a lively classic-rock tune.

"You! You're not dancing!" Malfruddin yelled, pointing at an onlooker by the door. "Keester, cut off his legs!"

But the fleshopod made no reply. He was too busy staring at his designated victim: the former owner of Pinkie's, the traveling companion of Harlan and Melvinge, Keester Button's very own parent/brother, the original to Keester's copy— in other words, Sid, who had followed Melvinge into the Dance Hall to watch the show, and hadn't ducked out of sight in time.

Sid stared back. He'd almost forgotten the loss of his original head-shaped pseudopod to Sdark (the new head was just as good, or even better), and he'd never had any inkling that within the Loan Shark's gullet his partial self might regenerate and grow. The last thing he'd expected to find in the Really Big Dance Hall, in fact, was a ready-made long-lost brother, and the unexpected confrontation left him frozen speechless.

Fatally, as it turned out. While Sid was still staring, Keester mobilized his own startled protoplasm, and hurried across the dance floor to enfold his clonesibling in a warm—and absorbing—embrace.

"There's room for just one fleshopod in this Parking Lot," Keester shouted, squeezing his clonesibling tightly, "and it's going to be Keester Button!"

He was right, as it turned out—but only half right. For in the instant that Keester made contact with his clonesibling Sid, the irreversible process of absorption began. What Keester hadn't expected was that the process, once started, would work both ways. At the same time Sid was becoming one with Keester Button, Keester was becoming one with Sid.

"Hey, wait a minute!" Keester yelled, as the two amorphoid fleshopod bodies began to fuse together, going from something (or a pair of somethings) more or less human-looking to something that looked like a beanbag chair with convulsions. "Stop! Can't we talk this ov—!"

His mouth disappeared into the lump of amorphoid protoplasm, and the yelling ceased.

Chapter 21

Larry Ties Up a Few Loose Ends

Melvinge's gonna find the Mall
    He ain't found it yet.
Gonna lead the folks and all,
    But he ain't found it yet.

—Blind Grapefruit

Everybody in the Really Big Dance Hall stared at the lump of protoplasm that had once been Sid and Keester Button. It wasn't moving.

"Is it dead?" asked Loola.

Nobody answered her. Finally Melvinge stepped forward and poked at the blob with one finger. It gave a little under his touch, with a sort of gurgling feeling like a plastic garbage bag filled with Jell-O. When he took his finger away, the dent he'd left stayed for a moment before it disappeared.

"I don't think so," he told Loola.

Harlan came forward (he'd been hiding near the door all this time, trying to avoid the notice of Sdark and Keester Button) and prodded the blob with the toe of his boot.

"Maybe it's not dead, boss," he said to Melvinge, "but I'm not certain it's alive, either."

Malfruddin—he of the geeky eyebrows and mysterious, deep-laid plans—pushed his way to the front of the little crowd of onlookers.

"It's gotta be one or the other," he informed the dogoid. "Because if it's alive then it's passed out cold on my dance floor, and I want it thrown out on its ear for creating a disturbance, blocking traffic, and committing a merger in public. And if it's dead it's trash, and I want someone to haul it to the dump."

The dogoid looked from Malfruddin to his boss. Melvinge shrugged.

"Beats me," Melvinge said. "But it looks too heavy for one person to carry. Maybe if we just leave it alone, it'll get bored and ooze away."

"No," said Malfruddin.

In the same instant, a voice from the doorway of the Really Big Dance Hall cried out, "Lo!"

Standing at the door were Herk and Bare. Only prophets, stage magicians, and certifiable lunatics can shout things like "Lo!" in public and sound like they're serious. Herk and Bare pushed their way through into the Dance Hall at the head of a crowd of zealots—some in genuine Bare-shirts, some in fake Bare-shirts, and a few freethinking spirits in blue-and-yellow Hawaiian numbers like Herk's.

"Lo!" exclaimed Herk again. "Behold! The True Hero and Prophet has been revealed!"

To Melvinge's astonishment,[1] Herk pointed straight at the lump of protoplasm that had

[1] Not to mention the astonishment of Loola, Harlan, Malfruddin, and everybody else who'd been in the Dance Hall when the crowd of cultists showed up—with the exception of Don Boethius and the Consolations, who'd been playing gigs in the Parking Lot for so long that nothing ever astonished them anymore.

formerly been Sid and Keester Button.

"I'm not certain—" Melvinge began.

"He is dead," Herk said firmly, "and he is not dead. Is that not so?"

Melvinge shrugged. "That's one way to put it."

"And furthermore," said Bare, "he only has one ear."

"He hasn't even got that much," Melvinge said.

"I dunno, boss," said Harlan. "Come around and look at it from this angle."

Melvinge walked around the lump of protoplasm and stood next to Harlan and the two visionaries. The dogoid had spoken the truth. Here was the lobe, there was the shell . . . indeed, as Herk would have said, and lo!—from this side of the lump, the smooth curve of pseudoflesh appeared to be one huge, slightly cauliflowered ear.

"You have a point there," Melvinge said to Herk and Bare.

"Indubitably," said Bare. "The ancient texts were, after all, quite specific."

"And as added proof," Herk said, "need I point out that the True Hero and Prophet is, like my friend here, bare?"

"I guess not," said Harlan. He scratched himself behind one ear with his hind foot (a habit of his, when puzzled or confused) and said, "Just one thing, guys. You told me that your hero or prophet or whatever was going to lead everybody to the Megaverse Mall. But as far as I can see, he didn't get any further than this two-bit Dance Hall."

"Hey, wait a minute!" yelped Malfruddin. "Just whose Dance Hall are you calling 'two-bit,' you mangy half-hound!"

"I am *not* mangy!" snarled Harlan, and a brawl might well have commenced if the Earring of Erk had not once again prompted Melvinge to a burst of clever deviousness.

"I've got it!" he shouted, loudly enough to make himself heard over Harlan and Malfruddin's rising exchange of insults. "I understand everything— the real meaning of the Really Big Dance Hall, and why Sdark wanted to close it down! The True Hero and Prophet was right!"

Everybody stared at Melvinge. Loola looked impressed by her new-found True Love's unexpected insight. Harlan looked skeptical. Malfruddin looked suspicious. Even Herk and Bare looked startled—they weren't used to the idea of other people having revelations while they were around.

"It's like this," Melvinge continued in a hurry. "We know that Sid . . . uh, Keester . . . uh, Sidandkeester, here, is the True Hero and Prophet, because of the signs that you two gentlemen have pointed out to us. And we know that the True Hero and Prophet was destined to find the Megaverse Mall. Since what Sidandkeester found was the Really Big Dance Hall, then obviously—"

He paused for effect. Everybody was still staring at him. He went on.

"Then, obviously, the Really Big Dance Hall is, in fact, and in spite of its surface appearance, actually and indubitably the Meg-Universal Mall!"

Harlan scratched behind his ear again. "I don't get it, boss."

"*I* understand it!" cried Loola. From the light in her dark and only slightly reptilian eyes, revelations were going for a dime a dozen on the dance floor tonight. "The Megaverse Mall is all about buying and selling, and whenever we buy and sell anything—dances, Fudgesicles, little carved jade trinkets—then we have the Megaverse Mall within us. What we have to do now is build the Mall ourselves, right here amid the rusty autos of the Parking Lot!"

A shout of agreement rose up from the troop of zealots who'd come into the Dance Hall with Herk and Bare. Melvinge clasped his gypsy beloved in an admiring embrace. Harlan shrugged, and joined in the cheering with the rest. Herk, Bare, and their followers crowded around the protoplasmic mass of the True Hero and Prophet Sidandkeester, and with massive displays of effort lifted it up and bore it out of the Dance Hall into the Parking Lot. There, with some help from Ojibway Khartoum and the Motorcycle Monks, they enshrined it on the roof of an abandoned schoolbus.

Malfruddin, unnoticed in the commotion, smiled quietly to himself.

Some distance away, in a Gypsy encampment, a woman with a henna-red beehive hairdo and rhinestone sunglasses watched the events at the Dance Hall on an antique black-and-white crystal ball set. The picture faded out as the inhabitants of the Parking Lot began decking the shrine of the True Hero and Prophet Sidandkeester with garlands of paper flowers—but not before the scene cut quickly to a one-eared man in a floppy hat, standing apart and fingering the hilt of an old-fashioned saber.

"Rrruff?" said the werewolf that crouched on the rug beside the woman's rocking chair.

She bent down and unfastened the collar around the werewolf's neck. "You can change back now," she said. "This part of the story is over."

The werewolf didn't say anything, but dashed away into the curtained-off back of the gypsy wagon. A couple of minutes later, Larry Halibut came out again, this time in his normal (if not very imposing) human guise. He was dressed in a faded purple housecoat many sizes too large for him.

"You've got to find me some new clothes," he said to the woman, who no longer had red hair and sunglasses, but wore instead the colorful garments of a Gypsy Queen. "I don't know where I left the old ones. Say, Novaleen—was it Ratner we saw there at the end?"

"It sure was," said Ruth, aka Novaleen. "He blames Melvinge for turning Malfruddin against him."

"That could cause trouble later," Larry said.

"Oh, it certainly will," Novaleen agreed. "And Sdark has only been temporarily defeated, and Malfruddin has evil plans of his own. Poor Melvinge has a lot of work to do before he finds the true Meg-Universal Mall."

"One thing I still don't understand," said Larry,

who as a part-time novelist had a storyteller's compulsion to tie up all the loose ends. "We were the ones who shot Melvinge with a silver bullet and killed him in the first place. Why did we do it—and then go through all that trouble to bring him back to life?"

Novaleen smiled. "For the sake of the learning experience, dearie."

"Yours?"

"No," said Novaleen the Ruthless. "His."

Afterword

Some of it comes back to me. The last thing I remember clearly was a dinner party at the home of this rich guy—a publisher, I think it may have been. Some big estate in Westchester County. I had to take a train and then was met at the station by the publisher's chauffeur. At the house there were a lot of people I didn't know. I had the feeling everybody was looking at me, watching me at the dinner table.

After that it's mostly a blur. For a long time I remembered nothing. It was completely by chance that Bob Winston, a friend of mine, in town for a couple of days on a buying trip for a frozen beef concern in Alaska, recognized me stumbling around lower Manhattan. I'd been missing for weeks. Bob somehow knew it was me, though I was caked with dirt and had lost seventy pounds. I didn't know him, and when he took me to my home, I didn't recognize my wife. I was put in

149

the Psychiatric Ward at St. Francis Hospital in Jersey City for eight weeks, during which time my physical health improved, and my confusion diminished slightly.

When I was released, I still wasn't sure of my own name half the time. I spent more weeks at home, sitting in the laundry room tearing copies of *The New York Times* into strips, and fashioning huge nests into which I would crawl, and make whimpering sounds.

My mother, a wealthy widow living in California, cashed in some stocks and arranged for me to be brought to Buenos Aires to the private clinic of Dr. Ernesto Ryan. Here, an extensive assessment of my condition was undertaken. Dr. Ryan, a charming man who speaks to me in Spanish with an Irish lilt, supervised my first days personally. Everything was done to make me comfortable. I was even supplied with fresh copies of the airmail edition of *The New York Times* to facilitate the making of my nest.

At the time of my arrival, I was in very poor shape. I tended to go rigid for days at a time. Periodically, I would ramble incessantly about Italian ices—but when these were brought to me, I would shriek with horror and dive for my nest of shredded newspaper. In calm moments, I would stare vacantly, hum snatches of Schubert lieder, and drool. With expert care, daily sessions with a therapist and Dr. Ryan's amazing all-beef diet, I have been improving steadily, to the extent that I have even been given a typewriter, and allowed to work in my room for four hours a day—two hours in the morning and two hours in the afternoon before my empanada break. I remember that I earned my living as a writer before the incident.

The incident. That part is still pretty murky. There was the dinner party, by the end of which I was hallucinating heavily. Clearly, some sort of drug had been introduced into my food, and I had customarily eaten more than my share.

In the sixties I had shunned the psychedelic drugs so popular at the time, and had no firsthand knowledge of LSD trips and the like—however, my experiences at the party were not unlike those described by my acid-dropping friends. The other guests, most of them, seemed to have vanished, and the remaining people—three or four of them—appeared to have suited up in surgical greens.

Then I have some vague recollection of being transported on a rolling stretcher. I may have been taken in an ambulance—maybe I remained in the house of the publisher. I do recall being rolled aboard an elevator.

Now my recall becomes even more fragmented and jumpy. I do not wish to horrify or upset the reader, nor to put undue strain on my own nervous system, which is still fragile and in a state of recovery, so I will not attempt to characterize the distortions of reality and caprices of the mind that afflicted me at this time. Save this: An African Crested Crane, named Egon, appeared at my bedside more than once, and conversed with me.

I liked Egon, and looked forward to his visits. Clearly he was in league with my captors—I understood that I was being held captive—and was able to visit me only with their knowledge and permission. Still, he was amusing and friendly, had an endless store of funny anecdotes and, with his beak, would inject me with a drug similar to morphine, which had the effect of steadying my nerves. Egon was, I somehow know, a retired Army Psychiatrist named Lewis, and not an African Crested Crane at all—but I only remember him in that form.

The others who moved fuzzily in and out of my consciousness during the period were mostly in medical garb. I know I was anesthetized a number of times, and operations were performed without my consent. Evidence of one of these is a pair of gold-plated RCA jacks, identical to those on the back of your stereo, which have been implanted in my left temple. X-rays made here at Dr. Ryan's clinic clearly show a network of near-microscopic wires which have been intricately woven into some of the major neural centers—but to what purpose, and what sort of device was meant to be attached to those jacks, Dr. Ryan is at a loss to explain.

That is practically the sum of my conscious recollection of the period preceding my discovery on Great Jones Street in New York, and subsequent transportation to Buenos Aires.

But it is not all that is known. With my permission a microphone was placed in my room, and my every moment was monitored and taped. From my first night in Dr. Ryan's clinic, it was discovered that I spoke extensively in my sleep. Much of

152

what I said was gibberish, but certain significant words and phrases tended to be repeated, and snatches of what appeared to be remembered conversations, with Egon and others, could be assembled into a fabric which almost made sense.

Every few days, Dr. Ryan and I would listen to edited versions of my nocturnal speeches, and those versions would be added to further tapings, similarly condensed, until a rough scenario began to emerge.

From my various mumblings, strangled cries, and occasional lucid speeches Dr. Ernesto Ryan and I pieced together the story of a crime so diabolical that I wonder whether the reader will credit it. All the details of my recent indisposition—or to be blunt, madness—would argue against such an account being anything but one more paranoid delusion. That, of course, is the fiendish cleverness of the scheme.

I can only present the facts, believe them if the reader will. My captors, of course, had lured me to the dinner party for the sole purpose of drugging and abducting me. The other dinner guests were all accomplices.

Once I was in their power, the fiends had RCA jacks surgically implanted, and then connected me to some unheard-of computer capable of extracting and interpreting creative thoughts from my very brain.

By means of drugs, insinuations, and suggestions, these monsters may have caused me to helplessly divulge who knows what plots, outlines, schema, novellas, skits, essays, jokes, sermons, screenplays, double-crostics, limericks, puns, romances, epics, lampoons, commentaries, histories, encomia and festschrifts. Also allegories, bildungsromans, apothegms and analects. Plus comics, thrillers, dime novels and penny-dreadfuls.

Once they had drained me of a lifetime's output of literary work, they dumped me on the streets of Manhattan to wander, three-quarters-crazy, perhaps to starve and die. Then, these monsters would have their computer execute the various literary works or perhaps farm them out to other writers who'd fallen under their evil power.

Of course, with my shattered memory I have no way of knowing, for example, what contracts I may have signed with honest publishers—so it would be a simple matter for the kidnappers to create literary contracts which, without doubt, I would have signed.

Dr. Ryan, anxious for me to begin earning my living again, has advised me simply to honor whatever contracts I may be presented with, and not worry overmuch how they came about.

So, in the present case, this volume—which appears to be based on some outline or notes written by me, although I have no recollection of ever doing such a thing—requires of me that I write some introductory material.

I can't say as a matter of certainty that the scheme for this book was sucked out of my agonized brain by villainous high-tech literary pirates. Maybe it was, maybe it wasn't. Maybe during my days of stumbling around the streets of

New York subsisting on fortified wine, I actually did write something and sign papers. There's no way of knowing. I looked over the manuscript, and didn't recognize anything in it.

—Daniel M. Pinkwater